The Haunting of Oakwc
And other Storie
By Gail Lawler
Copyright 2022

A collection of short stories written over the last 10 years.

Dedicated to my mum.

Amor Omnia Vincit – Love conquers all

The following short stories are a collection written over the last 10 years. They are mainly experimental pieces -all about finding my voice as a writer – trying different styles and genres. On first attempts, I thought this book would be a random selection, but on re-editing- I find many similar themes emerging. I hope readers of this book find something they enjoy within the pages.

Gail

CONTENTS

The inspiration for this story comes from many holidays in Italy and visits to countless rural churches like the one described in the story. There's a simplistic beauty about them that I find inspiring, and I've always been fascinated by the religious effigies and countless tales of miracles

COMMUNION

The little church of Maria Sant Adavulgio stood high amid the olive trees, perched on a hillside overlooking the Great Lake.
The white scarred walls blistered by the heat reflected the sun and made a beacon of the edifice, guiding visitors up the rugged slope to the open door.
The little church was never closed, and the postcard beauty ensured it was rarely empty.

That was my first impression and one I will never forget.

We were on our honeymoon in Italy, and I was the happiest I'd ever been. Alex was close by my side, his right hand held softly against mine, assisting me gently as though I was the most precious thing in the world.

The wedding had taken place in a picturesque village church in Yorkshire, his home, not mine. My parents were both long dead, and relatives few. The day had been glorious -an early summer day full of promise, sunlight, and rose blossom.

Alex stood next to me, his hand shaking slightly as he slipped the fine gold band on the fourth finger of my left hand. As the church bells rang out, I remember my father-in-law whispering close in my ear, reminding me to listen to their joyous peal, to capture the brief moment before it was lost.

I can hear them now, tumbling and dancing across the vast expanse of Yorkshire moorland.

A perfect day.

And now we were here - a quaint, picturesque town in Northern Italy, hand in hand, breathing in the sweet clear air.

Was it possible to be so perfectly happy?

We had first seen the church on our way to the small pensione, booked for the ten days of our honeymoon. Travelling through the rural landscape, I'd seen the church, a flash of white through the gnarled trunks of ancient olive groves and tangled vineyards. The beauty and semi solitude drew my eyes until the image became embedded, its outline flickering behind my closing eyelids.

The family-owned hotel was small and intimate. The host Georgio and his wife treated us like royalty. Nothing was too much to ask. We ate the delicious food, home-cooked by Maria, and drank the sweet and full-bodied wine particular to that region.

The days seemed endless, and we rarely strayed far from our pretty base. We roamed the landscape taking photographs of the remote villages, sipping endless coffee under the bright, azure canopy.

My thoughts strayed back to the white church on the penultimate day of our honeymoon. Alex returned from his morning walk with a small bouquet of wildflowers that he produced with a schoolboy flourish.

Over breakfast that morning, he asked what I would like to do. At first, I didn't know and didn't care. The last eight days had been idyllic, and anything we did together sublime. It was then the picture of the little church flashed through my mind. I could see it clearly, perched high among the olive trees.

We made enquiries to Georgio. Unfortunately, my directions were vague, having only seen the church briefly en route to the hotel. However, with my scant description, Georgio was confident it was Maria Sant Adavulgio, an ancient and beautiful church famous for its miracles.

A young girl had seen a vision during the second world war - the Madonna had spoken and blessed her. Ever since the place had been a shrine for those seeking solace and healing.
The story only added to the attraction, and although quite a drive away, we set off after breakfast to miss the heat of the day.

The sun was already rising, and with the promise of temperatures in the 40s, we opened the car windows to enjoy the fresh breeze as we sped along the twisting rural roads. I was carefree for a few miles, yet looking out across the countryside, there was a sudden shift in my mood, a distinct catch to my happiness as if it was too perfect to last.

Maybe it was the realisation that the honeymoon was almost over, or that suddenly finding my happiness complete, something was wanting. Would the rest of my life be a pale imitation of this moment?

Alex reached over and squeezed my knee, bringing me back to my senses. I smiled and yawned, shrugging off my lowering spirits to the breeze.

'Soon be there.'

There was no road up to the church, and we parked the car at the bottom of the hill, luckily in the shade.
The approach was steep, and the church further away than it looked, but the walk would be good after the overindulging of the past week

We set off up a track, well-worn and travelled. The path was dry and dusty, the earth a deep terracotta. My sandals were open at the front, and the red dust settled between my toes. Alex teased me for wearing inappropriate footwear as I held onto his arm, using his strength to propel me up the slope.

By now, the sun had risen to its zenith. I could feel the sweat on my body beneath the thin cotton dress and bead across my brow. My legs grew heavy as I tugged on Alex's arm. The track was in direct sunlight, with no comforting shade of olive trees.

Alex looked cool in a short-sleeve shirt and shorts and hadn't even broken into a sweat. He smiled down at me and wiped my brow with his handkerchief in mock chivalry. We were about halfway to the church, and I wished I'd brought my sun hat. I could feel the sun burning into my scalp and my temples tightening.

We set off again, and I tried to quicken my steps to reach the sanctuary of the church before the heat overwhelmed me.
I must have started to tire, for Alex's arm became a burden, tugging instead of supporting me up the hill. Releasing my hold, I lagged behind, almost crawling up the slope while Alex disappeared ahead. He shouted down to me –now hidden beyond the bend - a faceless voice promising to wait at the top.

I thought miserably of how he would have stayed with me only a few days earlier. Was this a sign of things to come – romance already withering?

Stopping to wipe my brow, I took a deep breath before striding purposely to the top.

Alex sat beneath an olive tree, laughing at my predicament. I didn't see the funny side. Hot and bothered, soaked with sweat, and with the beginning of a migraine, I felt cross and wasn't in the mood for teasing. Would this be the first row of our married life?

My husband stood and came forward, gently taking my hand and running his fingers through my hair. The tenderness of the moment overwhelmed me for a moment. Breathing hard to keep my feelings in check, I took his hand, and in silence, we walked to the church.

The age of the building became apparent as we approached the open door. It was patched with amateur repairs, the paint peeling and cracked. A single tower rose to one side, and as we stepped inside, the bell began to toll midday.

The coolness and shade were an immediate welcome, the hallowed and hushed air bringing peace from the afternoon glare. My body felt limp, and my eyes, still dazzled by the bright sun, danced with flashes of orange and white.

Feeling dizzy, I leaned on Alex to steady myself and looked around.

The inside of the church was breathlessly simple. It contained an unearthly beauty that caused an ache within my heart that was neither joy nor unhappiness.

The walls were bare stone, and even the glass windows unstained. It was the beauty of the altar, however, lit by a single shaft of light, that caught my gaze.

Adorned with wildflowers from the surrounding countryside, the altar took my breath.

Hundreds of tiny candles flickered amongst the petals and foliage, the light dancing upon the gilding as the flames quivered with every shift in the air.

In an alcove high above the altar stood a carving of the Madonna and the Christ child. The face of the Madonna was exquisite, the eyes wide and open, full of forgiveness and hope as they gazed upon the child staring upright in her wooden arms.

A murmur of voices caught my attention. I hadn't noticed the group at the front of the church until now. They appeared to be an Italian family, mother, father, and three children. The younger children, two boys, sat on either side of the parents. The oldest, a girl, sat at the front of the altar in a wheelchair.

I wondered how far these people had come, struggling to push the young girl uphill in the heat of the day.

The daughter seemed severely disabled. Her head lolling to one side, one arm twisted cruelly as she stared into the darkness.

I couldn't take my eyes off the poor girl, her head twitching and eyes wandering through the gloom. Then, just for a moment, her gentle, brown eyes locked onto mine -before moving involuntarily away again.

My head had started to pound—the effects of heatstroke, and moving towards the altar to take a photograph, a sudden dizzy spell took hold, as though a black shutter veiled my eyes

. . .

I must have fainted clean away. Everywhere ached -my neck sore, body twisted. Slowly, I opened my eyes - everything was hazy. The Madonna smiled down at me, hands wide in compassion, yet the Christ child was no longer with her. I opened my mouth to call Alex, but no sound came. Panicking, I tried to look around, but instead, my head rolled to one side.

I could see my body contorted, my right arm twisted, and a hand no longer my own but deformed and claw-like.
Trying to speak -I opened and closed my mouth, my tongue dry and swollen. I attempted to call again, but my words became unintelligible groans. A hand reached down to wipe away the spittle that had started to run from my lips. I looked for Alex, but all I could see was the face of the Italian woman who spoke to me in a language I did not understand, her eyes sad and afraid.

My head jerked to the right. It was then that I saw them, Alex and a woman. I had to close my eyes and open them again before the awful realisation suddenly dawned – that woman was me! Alex stroked the woman's hair, kissing her softly on the forehead and whispering soft words.

But it wasn't me. How could it be? I was here, twisted and deformed, trapped in a wheelchair at the front of the church…?

As I watched, the woman turned her face towards me and smiled – a look of hope in her eyes. I had seen those brown eyes before. Mine, yet not mine.

Almost choking with panic, the bile clogged my throat. I was trapped and attempted to cry out. Yet all I could manage was a roll of my eyes, my hand trembling.

I needed Alex to see me –for him to know what was happening. What if he left me here like this? Summoning my strength, I pushed and strained against the confines – eager for release.

The eyes of the Madonna looked on – gazing kindly into mine. My head ached – the lights from the candles flickering and flashing around me. I had to get back to Alex.

The wheelchair finally started to move, toppling forward. With one final effort, I managed to roll my body. I was finally breaking free…

• • •

It seemed as though I had lain on the floor for some time. My eyes were still closed – afraid to open, and my head pounding. Finally, I felt a kind and gentle touch against my cheek, wiping my brow, a voice reaching out through the darkness.

Alex stood above me, his face full of love and concern. As our eyes met, he knelt down and gently kissed me.

I had fallen, it seems, at the front of the church, fainted for a few moments. Trying to get my bearings, a sense of what had happened, I looked around, my eyes drawn to the myriad of tiny lights flickering amongst the flowers. Never had I felt so grateful for being alive, for being in love.

• • •

A light breeze entered the church of Maria Sant Adavulgio as the wooden Madonna looked out over the altar and smiled.

The End

The Secret of the Dragon Chair

The grieving lasted for months. It hung idly from clock hands and unwashed hair, lying thick in columns of dust, caught in the decay of weak afternoon sun.

It had been the edge of winter when he died, and now spring had erupted around earth's lifeless corpse bringing rebirth, but she could feel no joy.

Her mind had stopped. Thoughts car crashed against a wall of emotional pain that she could not scale, only sit and watch each second shift its tiny arm, ticking towards the day when she would join him.

Yet pain wears out the sufferer, and although the emptiness continued, her body grew restless for the usual routine, a betrayal to his memory.

The day started clear and bright. One single imprint of a star clung flatly against the blue curtain of morning. She wrestled with the fastening on her watch, finding the catch awkward and fiddly. He had bought it for her, and now it dangled loosely on her thin wrist, glinting in the early light.

Today would be the beginning. She would try to carry on as best she could without him. She would venture into his room and make a start.

The door to his office was shut. She pushed it gently and walked through, the stale, closed air rising to greet her. The curtains were pulled to, the room shadowy and just as he had left it. It had been his study, but in the last months of illness, a place of quiet contemplation to try and understand, if not totally accept, his fate.

The floor was littered with books ranging from Buddhism to Islam, Christianity to Atheism, a quest to know, a thirst for knowledge, a reassurance.

She wondered if he had found it in the end.

His chair stood by the window, and its emptiness made her sorrowful. In the last weeks, she had often entered quietly to find him asleep, tiptoeing in silence not to disturb his brief moments of peace.

She opened the curtains. The view from the window was the best in the house, overlooking the large garden and fields and woods beyond.

He had loved the outdoors. His final weeks had brought with them the constraints of an invalid, confining him to spend his last days behind walls. And so he had sat in this chair and gazed longingly at his beloved countryside. She had tried to brighten the room, bringing the outdoors in, filling the room with flowers and greenery, but the shop-bought plants were a weak imitation of nature.

And now it was spring, his favourite time of year. Often he had woken early, setting off in the crisp morning air, walking the dog to greet the sunrise rolling in over the expansive hills to the east.
He would always be back just as she awoke with a cup of tea in one hand and a bunch of wildflowers in the other. A bouquet of buttercups, daisies, wild primrose, and forget-me-nots.

But that was before.

Sitting in the chair, she closed her eyes. How long would this pain last? She sank into it, her body tired from sorrow.

It was a beautiful chair, an antique made from Japanese Oak. He had bought it on his travels to the East. The back of the chair was exquisitely carved in the shape of two dragons.
He had called it 'The Dragon Chair,' an enchanted piece made for a Japanese crown princess over 4 centuries ago – a gift from her husband as a symbol of eternal love.

It reminded her of an old Enid Blyton book she had read as a child - *'The Wishing Chair.'*

Maybe if she wished hard enough, this pain would end...

The sun had risen and moved westward across the sky, falling full-beam into the room. The dusty surfaces absorbed the light flatly, powdering the space like a pause in time.

Weary from weeks of grief, she let her head gently slip towards her chest, and soon she was asleep.

She dreamt, and he was with her.

Waking, her mouth was dry, and her neck sore. Lifting her head, she tilted it back and forward to relieve the stiffness. She looked at her watch. It was almost noon, and the sun had left the room. She was alone again. Her hands rubbed against the smooth surface of the chair arms.

So many lifetimes.

The golden hue of the ancient wood gleamed intact, its warmth and heart still alive, still breathing. Had he believed in the hope of Resurrection? She could not believe it. There was no hope. Nothing remained.

Pressing down on the chair arms to help her stand, the wood gave way slightly beneath her hand. Lifting her arm, she saw the wood indented where her arm had rested.

Letting her fingers run over the worn surface, her nails caught in the line of a rectangular compartment set into the wooden frame. She hadn't noticed it before and, feeling the edges with her fingertips, tried to pull it open towards her, but it held fast.

She tried again more forcibly until, in one bold move, a small, hidden drawer pulled away, scattering its secrets into the air.

She watched as the tiny dried blue flower heads drifted across her lap and into the dimming light.

Forget-me-not, she whispered into the shadows.

The End

I wrote this story many years ago during a snowstorm in the depth of winter. I like how a thick blanket of snow cuts everything off, and I wanted to portray a feeling of isolation.

Petre and Anna

Anna looked up from her mending to gaze for a few moments at her young husband. He'd been scribbling away for hours, sat at the table by the window to make the most of the diminishing light.

His brow creased as he poured over the words flowing slowly from the nib, blackbirds leaning against a white sky, straining for flight.

Occasionally he glanced from the paper at the outside world, the bitter reality of the stark winter night crashing against the glass. The moon, heavy and waxing, stared back. All was quiet bar the scratch of pen against paper, stopping and starting as each sentence was deliberated over, deleted, changed.

She loved him very much.

Throughout the winter, Petre worked all day and long into the night. His young wife watched, waiting for him to return to her, busying herself with sewing, cutting him slices of bread and cheese, keeping the meagre fire burning.
Often she had fallen asleep in her chair, waking to find Petre still writing many hours later.

With a loud sigh, Petre put down his pen. His young body was stiff from several hours of hunched writing. Rubbing at his tired eyes, he stretched and yawned. Then, rolling his shoulders backwards and forwards, he walked over to the fire's embers to warm his cold hands.

Anna put down her sewing and glanced up expectantly at her husband, her eyes widening, lips poised in anticipation.

"It is finished," announced Petre without emotion, all energy spent and contained within the pages of the manuscript now piled in a heap upon the table.

Tears sprang to Anna's eyes as she leapt to her feet, scattering the garment she had been mending onto the stone floor. She caught him up in her arms and embraced her husband, repeating his name over and over again, enjoying the sound it made on her lips.

Petre kissed her forehead gently and stroked her hair.

The novel was finally finished. It had been over a year since he'd first put pen to paper. Petre and Anna had only been married six months when he'd begun to write the first chapter. Poor Anna. The passion he'd shown his young bride had been consumed by his writing, leaving none for her. Yet she had been patient, she had waited, and, at last, he had returned to her.

Petre's face was tired. He needed to rest. Releasing his wife with a smile, he walked over to the bed and fell immediately into a deep sleep.

Anna arranged the coverlet about his shoulders to keep him warm. Petre was so handsome. She had loved him from the first. His face was thinner, the cheeks hollow. He'd been working too hard -the book had possessed him completely. At first, she had been jealous as if a mistress had taken him away, but she had gradually accepted it. They talked very little over the last six months, sharing only common pleasantries, small meals, and sleep.

But now it was over, and Petre, her Petre, would return.

Walking over to the table, Anna picked up one of the sheets. It was the title page. Anna read the words - 'Escape,' a novel by Petre Andovochek, running her fingers lightly over his name with pride.

She knew little of writing, had never read a book in her life, not even her husband's work, but she was proud, so very proud.
Her husband was a genius. Of this, she was sure.

He might not be good at farming or clever with his hands like some men in the small village, but Petre would go far. Far away from this poverty, with her, his wife, at his side.

Placing the sheet carefully back on the table so as not to disturb her husband, she sat back in her chair and fell asleep by the glow of the remaining embers.

The following day Anna was awoken by the bustling of her husband around the small room. He had made a fire and was busy sorting through items in a large holdall.

Anna rose silently and tiptoed behind him, grabbing him around the waist and kissing his hair.

Smiling good-humouredly, Petre kissed his wife on the forehead before releasing her arms. His face was bright and open, with no hint of tiredness from the previous evening.

"Anna, Anna, I must go to Moscow today to see Ivan Popov about my book. I must hurry. The train leaves in an hour," and with that, he turned his back and began to pack his belongings into a large woven bag.

Anna's shoulders sank as she stepped back towards the fire.

"Must you go today, Petre?" she asked in a small voice.

"Of course. I need to sell my work. Ivan Popov has promised me a handsome sum based on the first three chapters I sent him".

'But it is snowing, my love'?

Petre glanced out into the morning, the sky a yellowing grey, the snow falling thick and heavy.

"Ah, this is nothing. We have had much worse", he laughed, but seeing his wife's sad face, he put down the clothing in his hands and went to the fire to embrace her.

"Anna, I must do this. I have worked over a year for this, for us".

"How long will you be away"?

Petre looked down at his boots. The world was opening up to him; he was going to Moscow.

"I don't know, but it won't be long, a couple of weeks at most."

Anna's eyes filled, and she blinked quickly to steady the tears.

"You have enough money for food"? He asked.

"Yes, Petre."

"And you can call on Katria Novikov if you need anything"?

"Yes, Petre."

"Well, then, everything will be well, and I will come home a rich man. I will buy you anything you want. Perhaps a new dress, a new coat like the mayor's wife?"

"Perhaps, my love," Anna attempted to smile. Her husband was more precious to her than any amount of money. But he was ambitious, and she should not hold him back from his dreams with her own.

Petre embraced his wife quickly before moving back to the table.

"I must set off soon."

Anna watched as Petre put on his scarf, long coat, and gloves. Her heart was wretched, yet she smiled and wished him well.

Shouldering his holdall, Petre took her hand and kissed her gently. "Two weeks, my love. That is all. The time will pass quickly."

With that, he opened the large wooden door, stepped down the path, and out into the cold light.

Anna stood at the window and watched the dark figure crawl away over the white landscape. The flakes fell thickly, obscuring the tiny windowpane until all she could see was snow.

The End

I was asked to write and perform the following story for Wylam Winter Tales in 2021 – a fictional piece based on a true story. It was written in a style to be performed, and the original video has sound effects! The extract from the newspaper is an exact copy of the actual report of the event.

The Haunting of Oakwood Hall

I

I wake up -wet with sweat – my heart hammering. My husband Joe – sleeps like a babe beside me and doesn't stir. It's the third time this week I've woken from a dream. The same terrifying – heart-wrenching dream.
We've been through a lot over the last four years, and I don't want to disturb his peace.

Save the children.

A voice echoes inside my head – half-whispered like the last leaves falling in the silence of winter. Is it my own voice I hear or one dreamt up in the labyrinth of my disturbed mind?

It's cold – so very cold, and I pull the quilt tightly around my arms – seeking comfort in the warmth.

I've never been one for nightmares, even as a child - It's just since… we moved into this old place… Oakwood Hall – four months ago.

As soon as I walked through that old, heavy door, I could sense her.

It sounds ridiculous, but I know what I felt… the atmosphere thick and heavy – charged with unseen energy – like the air just before a storm. I shrugged it off at the time – laughed out loudly to frighten away any mischievous spirits and my own folly. I never mentioned it to Joe. He thinks I'm better – or at least better than I was.

But now I know what it was - who it was. She was there – waiting for me in the shadows.

Everything seems better in the daytime – even the shadows that creep across the bedclothes disappear with the morning sun. Mary is already awake – I can hear her running around in the playroom just down the hallway.

That's why we bought this rambling old house in the first place– space is such a luxury with a young family, and we aim to have more.

At least that was the idea when we married. After Mary's birth – four years ago – I became ill – not in the physical sense – but a disease of the mind – lacking that motherly bond with my own child – a mother's love.

I could never tell my husband the extent of my darkness – the horrible numbness - bereft of all feeling – the chill upon my heart at seeing my own daughter.

 I stretch and yawn, turning my face towards the early morning light, discerning the winter sun's wish–wash glimmer beyond the window.

Save the children

For a moment, the whispered words echo once again around my head. But there's no room for ghosts or daydreams, and pushing the thoughts aside, I quickly dress and go to Mary.

I listen at the door before I enter… the soft whispers as Mary talks to her dolls. She should have brothers and sisters to play with – not be an only child. It's all my fault…

Yet the sight of my daughter never ceases to amaze me – to think that this carefree angel is of my flesh.

Was I ever this happy?

As I open the door to her room – she runs to me – with a wide grin and chubby arms held wide to greet me. I go through the motions - pick her up and kiss her on the cheek with a heavy heart.

Will I ever feel the true bond between mother and child?

II

Later that afternoon, Mary is playing outside – muffled up in her hat and scarf against the cold. I watch her through the kitchen window as I clear away the breakfast things. The gardens a safe haven – and Mary loves to play with a plastic spade and bucket – digging up weeds and replanting them – only to dig them up once again.

My mind starts to drift – imagining the garden full of children playing happily in the sunshine – when a movement in the bushes breaks my gaze.

Suddenly, I feel terribly cold as my eye catches a black shape next to the old oak tree. It's a figure – or that's the impression I get - a woman clothed in a long black dress. I see a face – a deathly white face staring back at me -eyes black as night. I blink, and she's gone – only the tree with its branches swaying in the breeze.

 Instinctively I know it's her.

"Mary," – I rush to the door in a panic – feeling light-headed.

"Mary!"

Her tiny form comes running at her name.

"Mummy… - Algie picked these for you..."

She hands me a posy of ivy and other garden greenery.

Algie is Mary's invisible friend. He arrived at the same time we moved to Oakwood. The doctor says it's perfectly normal at her age – being an only child – spending days playing on her own.

I should try to do something about it, but she'll be going to school in less than a year, and Algie will be forgotten.

I usher her inside – my head throbbing and take one last look into the garden. The wintry sun is low, casting long dark shadows of trees across the lawn. It must have been the light playing tricks – the wind in the branches.

I close the door quickly on the dimming afternoon.

III

My headache lasts for the rest of the day. The prescription tablets don't even touch it, and by the time Joe arrives back home from work - I'm like a bear with a sore head, and I snap at him as soon as he steps through the door.

"Hey – what's the matter?"

He looks tired as he walks over to embrace me – but I turn away – cold to his warmth. I want to apologise – but the words won't come. Joe tries again, and I let his arms wrap around me – feel his energy. I want to tell him about what I saw today – but I remain silent.

Perhaps I'm still unwell?

For months after Mary was born, I saw things that nobody else could see – no sane person anyway. People long dead – not really ghosts – yet I saw their faces in the people passing me by in the street. The doctor prescribed pills to end the visions – but they emptied me out – until I was a shadow. It was no life.

Gradually – I weaned myself off them – thought I was cured, but now? Is it all starting again? Am I going mad?

My thoughts turn to my daughter and her invisible friend.

"I'm worried about Mary," I whisper.

Joe pulls away for a moment with a frown.

"Why – what's happened?" he asks.

"It's this imaginary friend…I… what if she's mad – like me?"

He cuts me off with a broad smile.

"You're not mad, love. You're doing fine. Algie? Oh, love. You had me worried there. Lots of kids have imaginary friends, and she'll soon grow out of it."

I'm not convinced.

"But it's such a strange name – Algie. I mean – how does a 4-year-old invent something like that?"

He gives me his bemused stare again.

"Algie – he's a character in that video she watches all the time– *The Little Princess*. Don't say you haven't noticed – she watches it all the time?"

I think for a moment and then start to laugh – until I can't stop. It's such a relief. Of course – Algie. That's where she gets the name from. I've been so silly – worrying.

IV

Later that night, I read Mary a bedtime story. She chooses one from her collection of Little Princess books. As we turn the pages, I point to one of the illustrations and decide to humour her.

"Look, Mary – it's Algie- your friend!"

She turns and gives me a bemused look that reminds me of her father.

"That's not Algie – mummy. He doesn't look like that at all – silly!"

She giggles and scrunches up her nose.

"Well, what does Algie look like?" I ask.

She laughs again. "Oh, mummy. Can't you see him? He's sat on the bed listening to the story."

She describes the imaginary boy at the foot of her bed. A young boy wearing a blue suit – short trousers and a jacket with a bow at the neck, long stockings, and lace-up boots in her own childlike way.

• • •

I don't sleep that night. There's a storm on the way, and the trees rattle and tap against the windowpane like some unquiet spirit trying to gain entry. Despite the cold, I get out of bed and walk to the window. The moon is high, casting the garden with an eerie luminescence. The dark trees and bushes writhe against the oncoming storms torment – twisting in agony. And then my heart freezes – as I see two dark shapes - a woman and a small boy turning their white, pale, almost translucent faces up towards me.

Save the Children

"No!!" I scream into the darkness as the light flicks on. Joe is at my side, and I fall into his arms.

"It's Ok, love. You were sleep-walking – that's all. You must have had a bad dream. It's ok – it's ok."

V

The next day I wake alone. Joe had an early start, and I listen a moment to the sounds of morning.

After the storm last night, all seems eerily quiet. The storm last night… an image of those two pale faces staring up at me…was it a dream?

I need to get out of this house – leave the shadows and ghosts of Oakwood Hall behind and feel the fresh Northumberland breeze in my hair.

After a hurried breakfast – I bundle Mary into the car and drive quickly away from the old stone walls. The sun is dazzlingly bright. It could be the middle of July if it wasn't for the leafless trees – standing stark against the skyline.

There's damage from last night's storm – limbs torn from trees and hedgerows as we pass. I switch on the radio, trying to bring some cheer – instead, I hear the local weatherman warning of more bad weather to come.

It's hard to imagine on a day like today- the calm before the storm, perhaps? I switch off the chattering voices, and we drive in silence – Mary lulled into sleep as I drive to nowhere in particular.

I've done little to acquaint myself with the local area. I drive past signs for Heddon on the Wall – Ponteland – East Wallhouses, and Matfen Village. I'm not interested in destinations – just driving.

I think I'm heading straight in one direction - but the twisty Northumberland roads are deceiving – and I pass another sign for Matfen Village. I turn the opposite way – but five minutes later – I pass another sign for Matfen.

A slight chill passes over my heart, and I shiver.

Do all roads lead to Matfen?

This is silly. Maybe I need to stretch my legs? I turn the car, and after about a minute, I see another sign, this time for Matfen Hall.

Matfen Hall. Something stirs inside my head like an old forgotten melody – but I shake away the feeling.

The Hall looms ahead - and I see it's now a hotel and health spa. I almost turn around- yet something keeps me driving onwards and into the car park. Now I'm here, I might as well take a look around. Perhaps I could visit the health spa sometime – it might do me good?

I park, and stepping from the car – I pull the coat tightly around me. Today, the sun is merely for decoration, and the air is bitingly cold. I shake Mary gently awake, not wanting to disturb her peaceful dreams – and putting on her hat and gloves, we step around to the front of the Hall.

The place is impressive – grand. I'm aware of the dark shapes of birds high in the trees that line the driveway as I stare up at the magnificent bayed front – and an overwhelming feeling of sadness washes over me.

I feel Mary's tiny hand inside my own and squeeze it tightly. There is something here – something dark and terrible. As my mood changes- so does the weather – the wind suddenly whipping around us – grey clouds gathering across the sun. I stare up at the grand stone edifice – dark mullioned windows reflecting the changing skies – all empty – except for one where a pale blank face looks down at me.

For a moment, I cannot move – fixed to the spot by some unearthly tie. The face is ghastly – white – a pitiful vision of sorrow. I'm aware of everything around me – feel Mary's hand leave mine as she runs, giggling towards the trees that line the driveway. I stand helpless – my eyes fixed on the spectre as the wind whips around me.

I'm conscious of the storm brewing – the trees shaking - a sudden squall causing a murmuration of rooks to rise and fall above me in black – screeching waves.

I close my eyes- shutting out the face at the window, and the noise intensifies. Above the birds cackling, I hear another sound – a horse and cart approaching. I open my eyes, the sound so near I fear being run into, but there is nothing.

Save the children.

"Mummy"!

I turn toward Mary as an almighty crack sounds through the air. I can see a small boy standing next to her, smiling. All I can do is watch as the wind loosens a bough from a tree high above her head and starts to fall.

"Mary!"

I scream, yet no sound comes. Instead, the noise of an oncoming cart fills my head – a horse whinnying and a woman screaming. I feel faint – my head spinning.

VI

I come to – propped on a plush sofa in what can only be the entrance lobby of Matfen Hall. A woman is smiling down at me.

"How are you feeling?"

My head feels thick – but I have only one thought.

"Mary?"

The woman smiles and turns her head. I follow her gaze, and there is Mary – sat opposite – swinging her chubby little legs.

"Mummy – you fainted!"

She runs into my arms, and I can't stop the tears from flowing. For once, my heart is full of motherly love.

"But what about the tree – the branch?"

Everything seems so muddled.

The woman looks confused for a moment.

"Oh yes – the storm – a few of the trees have been damaged…" she adds.

"But Mary - I saw the branch – it was falling …."

The woman shakes her head. "Mary's fine – she was playing near the doorway – or at least she was when I heard you call out and came running."

Mary giggles in my arms. "It was Algie – mummy. I was playing with Algie. His mummy came and was taking me inside. She seemed so sad."

VII

I never mentioned the incident to Joe – what could I say without sounding mad? Besides – after that day, I was filled with peace. Even Oakwood Hall seemed different – the air – lighter- free of the past.

I never saw the woman again. Never knew if it was all in my imagination.

That is until now – when repairs started on the old place – under part of the old floorboards – one of the builders found an old newspaper cutting. He gave it to Joe, who passed it on to me.

"Hey – look what's been found– I thought you would be interested?"

I take the yellowed paper fragment - the Newcastle Daily Chronicle – dated Thursday, October 1st, 1863.

I can feel my heart chill as I read the following.

Fatal Accident To Mrs Blackett Of Wylam.
A feeling of the deepest sorrow was caused in Wylam and the neighbourhood on Tuesday by the intelligence that Mrs Blackett, the wife of Capt. E.A. Blackett R.N of Wylam Oakwood had been killed by a fall from her carriage.

Mrs Blackett being a good driver, frequently drove out without attendants or any company, and on Tuesday, she, accompanied by two of her children (a boy about 11 years of age and a little girl), drove from Oakwood to Matfen Hall, the residence of Sier E A Blackett about 10 miles distant, in one of those low basket carriages that are now so fashionable.

Mrs Blackett and the children took luncheon at Matfen, and afterwards entered the carriage, intending to drive home by way of Stamfordham, where Mrs Blackett purposed to make a call. Scarcely had they taken their seats when the horse, a spirited bay of rather high breeding – became restive; and Mrs Blackett requested the children to get out of the carriage while she endeavoured to either conquer or calm the vicious brute.

They did so, but the horse continued to rear and plunge on the road through the shrubbery, and at last, the carriage upset, and Mrs Blackett was thrown with some violence to the ground. The gardener, who was at some distance, hastened to the assistance of the unfortunate lady and carried her to the house, but her head had been so severely injured that in a very few minutes after her removal to the entrance hall of the mansion, Mrs Blackett ceased to breathe. A family consisting of seven young children is left to deplore the loss of a most affectionate and estimable parent.

I read no more and let the paper slip from my hand and onto the floor.

• • •

Interested to know more – I search the internet for any further details of Mrs Lucy Blackett of Oakwood Wylam. I find the family tree on an ancestry website – all seven children listed.

At the bottom of the list - one name particularly catches my eye – Algernon Minchin Blackett 1862 – 1866. He was only one year old when his mother was so tragically killed – and four years when he joined her.

Affectionately known to his family as little Algie.

VIII

A week later, I stand in the grounds of St Mary the Virgin Church - Ovinghams graveyard and the final resting place of Lucy and Algernon Blackett.

Laying down a small wreath of flowers against the stone – erected in their memory – I give up a short prayer of thanks to Lucy for saving my daughter – but also for saving me.

May they rest in peace.

The End.

The title came first, then the ending, and the story followed. I had this image in my head… no spoilers!

Waiting for God

Sylvia shifted uneasily in her seat. The fake leather was cold, even beneath the thick layer of denim, and her warm breath steamed up the windscreen.
It had been Morris's idea, of course. Any self-respecting person would still be in bed, warm and unconscious. Her finger ends felt numb, hardly any feeling at all.
She rubbed them vigorously against her legs in the hope of restoring circulation.

Ridiculous weather for August.

She closed her eyes and tried to remain calm.

"A bit cold, Luv? It won't be long now."

Morris didn't even look up from his paper. Typical man. *He* was alright, padded jacket, gloves, flat cap. Oh, *he'd* made sure that *he* was nice and warm. If she'd known it would be this cold, she could have been better prepared and worn that scarf her youngest bought last Christmas.

When he said he'd take her out for an early morning run in the car, show her something special, she'd been intrigued.

She didn't expect many offers at 70, so however strange the request, she wasn't going to let the opportunity slip her by.

Even a trip out was a treat these days. Sylvia didn't drive, and since Ted died, there hadn't been that many excursions.

Every Sunday, come rain or shine, she and Ted had gone out for a run in the old VW. Had some lovely little drives, always stopping off somewhere for a bit of cake and a cuppa…

Now here she was… pre-dawn, stuck with Morris in the freezing cold.

She'd met him at the over 60's club. At first, she hadn't been bothered about joining in with the old fogies, but when Ted died, Sylvia felt lonely for the first time.

Coming from a large family and then looking after Ted and the three boys… the years had rolled away, full of noise and life. They'd passed too quickly, though. Even when it was just her and Ted, there'd been some fun in the house. Ted loved his records, and every day, just after lunch, he'd pop on one of the golden oldies, extend his hand, and they'd dance around the living room, eyes closed, back in their youth.

 Young at heart, that's what Ted had been, but of course, he wasn't.

It was his heart that finally gave up. Now the records gathered dust on the shelf, and Sylvia couldn't bear to play them - too many memories. Instead, she was left with the hollow sound of solitude.

She hardly ever saw the boys and their families. It was just at Christmas or her birthday, but then it was en masse. They all descended upon her in a heap of wives and grandchildren that she barely knew. Too much of a contrast to her regular routine, and she always sighed with relief when they left.

So when Morris walked into the village hall, her head had been turned by this striking, sprightly chap, looking much younger than his 74 years.

Morris had introduced himself, a widower of just one year. Later, when he'd asked Sylvia for a dance, she surprised herself by saying *yes*. Besides, there was no harm in a dance, and she enjoyed it.

He partnered with some of the other women but returned to her table after every dance. The conversation was limited, but it was nice to feel a man's attention again, even at her age.
So when he asked her out, she hadn't given it a second thought, even if it was at a ridiculous time in the morning.

And now, here she was, sitting in a freezing cold car at four a.m. It certainly wouldn't help her arthritis. Blowing on her hands to keep warm, Morris finally looked up from the paper.

'Cold Luv? Don't worry, I've got the very thing'.

Reaching into the back seat, Morris pulled out a carrier bag and took out a red tartan flask that offended Sylvia's eyes.

A Thermos, for God's sake!

Ted wouldn't have dreamed of bringing out a flask of tea.

"A proper brew out of a china cup," he would have said, *"none of this drinking out of a plastic cup for my Queen."*

They would have found a nice little tea room or cafe wherever they were and at whatever time.
Well, perhaps not at four in the morning, but Ted wouldn't have had such ridiculous ideas.

Apparently, Morris and his late wife had made the same trip every year. A special place, Morris said. Poor woman. Sat in a chilly car with only a thermos for comfort—no wonder she'd popped her clogs before him.

Still, Sylvia was cold and wouldn't say no to a cup of hot tea. Morris smiled as he handed her the flask and returned to his paper.

Not much company thought Sylvia as she unscrewed the lid and poured out a generous amount of the dark liquid, feeling the warmth permeate through the plastic cup and into her fingers.

Lifting the beaker to her mouth, she glugged down the warm brew – gagging immediately on the contents.
"Ewww," she just about managed to swallow the mouthful - the rest splashing over the rim of the cup and across her jeans.

It was Bovril. She hated Bovril. Now, as well as being cold, she had wet jeans and stank of the disgusting stuff.

Sylvia was at the end of her tether and started to wish she'd never bothered. Sat in a car in the middle of nowhere, on the edge of the moors, with a man she hardly knew. She must be mad. Never again!

She was just about to say as much, give Morris a piece of her mind, when he reached across and held her arm firmly, the newspaper falling onto his lap. He held a finger to his lips in silence.

Sylvia followed his gaze to a clump of trees no more than 50ft away from the car.

The light had just started to permeate the darkness, bringing a soft violet glow to the shadows. An early mist clung in the hollows and nooks as the spectre of morning approached.

And then it happened. There was a slight movement within the trees, branches swaying gently and the leaves whispering together as a shape appeared through the veil of the forest.

Sylvia forgot the cold, the wet jeans, the yeasty saltiness of the Bovril. She gazed in awe as a giant red stag revealed himself almost god-like in the early morning haze.

He stood proud, his head erect, the full antlers born like a magnificent crown as he gazed steadily, unblinkered, at the strange spectators.

And then he was gone.

For a moment, all was silent, a comfortable kind of silence. Sylvia turned to Morris. She hadn't realised he'd been crying, large soundless tears rolling down his cheek, gathering beneath his chin to drop softly onto his padded coat.

Reaching across, Sylvia tucked her cold hand beneath his arm as they sat in the peace of the early morning, waiting for the arrival of the sun.

The End

The idea for this story came when visiting friends many years ago. They lived in a beautiful part of the world with a vast rock-like hill near their home, visited by many climbers. They climbed it regularly and thought of it as their own. It almost became one of the family and was regarded with much affection

The Rock

The landscape lay flat for miles around, or if not flat, then gently undulating, lapping calmly across the lower slopes of the moors and wilderness beyond.

The only exception was the rock rising angular and distinct, a dark mass against the skyline.

Helen looked out into the night. A deep frost covered the land, and it shimmered, reflecting back the surface of a thousand stars. This was her home or had been for the last thirty years until now. Tonight was the last night she would spend in this spot before living in the city.

Soon she would be married and living with Ed, and this place, this night, would be a memory.

She'd been so sure up to this moment. Maybe it was last-minute nerves? The night was so beautiful, spreading its black velvet cape above her, a rich spangled web of stars and planets. But the heaving mass of eternity weighed heavy tonight. Beneath the heavens, she felt small and lost. Afraid of the future as the past peeled slowly away – from all she knew and loved.

There was Ed, of course. The man she loved. Ed.

She'd met him only six months ago, and he'd swept her off her feet. He was handsome - 6ft something with brown hair and matching eyes, a bad taste in clothes but a beautiful smile. He read poetry and the Classics, played rugby and squash, and liked the Rolling Stones. He was a Zoologist by profession, a caring, gentle man.
And she'd fallen, not in a slow-burning way, but in a whirl of sights, sounds, lips, and bodies mingling to become one with her life.

Usually, she'd been so steady in her ways. But, Ed had taken her by surprise- removed her guard in an unexpected moment. They'd met at a mutual friend's wedding, under the headiness of champagne and canapés, and drifted into a cosy bubble called love.

That is until now. Alone, looking out into the night, a sadness pervaded her happiness. The view before her was stamped clearly upon her heart, but perhaps only now did she fully appreciate it.

She'd been born here, taken her first steps, climbed trees, and scoured hedgerows for berries. Furthermore, she'd dreamed here of love, life, of days to pass. Now the future was upon her. Why did she feel such unhappiness?

Everything had been put in motion. Was it too late to back out now? Her belongings had been packed and sent into storage, and now she'd a few weeks doing her own thing while Ed worked away. She couldn't contact him, so remote was the place of his current work. So - she was going to freewheel for a while. It had seemed a good idea, but now she just felt lonely.

And the rock, *her* rock. She would miss it – but would it miss her? Helen peered into the night, her gaze resting on the dark mass, standing solitary and majestic in the moonlight. For all these years, the rock had been her shelter, escape, and confidant. It would be like leaving an old friend.

She needed to go there one more time, meditate on the future, and say goodbye.

Helen slipped on her walking boots, fleece, and jacket and headed into the cold night, the air relentless and unforgiving. Within minutes her features froze, the moisture on her lips cracking the delicate skin. It didn't matter. The outdoors was her second home. It was the only place she felt truly alive, and the fear within her started to ease

The hard ground popped under her tread, the imprints trailing behind her in the crisp frost as she made her way toward the rock.
It was made from millstone grit, coarse-grained sandstone of the Carboniferous age.

Folklore suggested that in ancient times – the wife of the great northern giant 'Rombald' had thrown rocks at her husband during a quarrel -and one of the stones had landed here.

Would she and Ed fight?

The rock measured 212 meters at its highest point and provided climbing to those seeking such sport.
But tonight, it was her rock and hers alone. Nothing else existed. Nothing else mattered. She would climb to her favourite spot, some 30 meters up on the western side. It was a gentle, sheltered climb known locally as *Lovers Leap*.

She smiled at the thought, amused by the name, for she had no necessity to jump for love; she was one of the lucky ones.

Helen started her climb, a route she'd taken hundreds of times before – but tonight, the ascent seemed difficult. She often scaled the craggy slopes in the moonlight but never on such a cold, cruel night.

Even in thermal gloves, her fingers were numb, and she could hardly feel the hard stone as she manoeuvred her hands and feet slowly upwards. Yet she knew this rock like a lover, the curves and sharp spaces, hollows, and curves until finally she reached the spot and stood for a moment to catch her breath.

It was so peaceful up here. That's why she loved it. No mobile phone signals, nothing to interrupt or disturb the quiet.

The view was amazing, even at night. She could see the twinkle of the streetlights in distant Harrogate and the dark lonely stretch of the North Yorkshire moors in the distance.

Somewhere under the heavens, the White Horse of Kilburn lay dreaming.

The night was exceptionally clear. The celestial bodies were at their brightest. Orion, the great hunter, the Big Dipper, and Ursa Major guiding her eyes to the North Star, the most brilliant and clearest of them all.

Then the grief started again, an ache gnawing deep within her. The sharp air plucked at her eyes, causing an overflow of emotion to stream over the wide brim of night.

Helen sat back in the ravine, her body and mind heavy with sleep and grief. Could she leave this place? Her body moulded against the stone, and she felt the solid protection of the rock caress her.

"My old friend," she whispered in a sob, "my old friend, how can I leave you?"

Running a gloved hand over the gnarled surface of the stone, she bent forward to lightly kiss the rough exterior with frozen lips, the tears salty against her mouth. She remained still for a few moments, arms wrapped around the granite - sobbing into the night.

The tears subsided after a while. She could feel the damp chill beneath the thick layers of clothing and shivered, arms goose pricked beneath the fleece. Looking up at the sky, the stars winked back, the waxing gibbous moon hanging heavy in exposure, the universe at peace.

This is how it should be.

The grief no longer belonged to her but scattered across the night. Her head was clear. The deep yearning for the girl she'd once been having passed. Soon there would be a new moon, a new beginning. The world would keep turning. She needed to live, be part of the world, and the rock would stay here constant, unchanged.

Helen smiled. How foolish she'd been. She loved Ed - how could she have doubted it? Later she'd phone her friends and arrange a get-together – it would be good to catch up.

Still smiling, she pushed herself up from the rock, arms frozen, eager to descend before the night frost set in.

Stepping from the hidden lair, her foot caught beneath the rocks, and she twisted, falling back into the ravine. Helen pulled at her foot, but it was trapped in a narrow crevice. The pain started to throb, and the harder she pulled, the worse it became. Placing her hands against the hard surface, she pushed with all her body weight, trying to lever her foot away, but the rock was unforgiving and would not give up its prize.

The hours passed, and darkness ebbed away towards morning. A light fall of snow drifted over the fields, covering her footprints, as the rock cast its shadow against the dawn.

The End

One of my favourite books (and writers) is The House on the Strand by Daphne du Maurier. I started to write something about time travel in the same vein, but it became this. I'm always amazed how a story changes shape as I write it...

The Time Machine

The room was perfectly white. It glistened with an intense cleanliness that dazzled the eyes. You couldn't get this clean without the aid of biological warfare. Surfaces scrubbed and scrubbed again, stainless steel and synthetic apparatus sterilised. The smell of hospitalisation lingered, a blend of surgical disinfectant and soap everywhere.

But this wasn't a hospital. It was a small laboratory within the Newcastle university faculty for genetic experimentation.

Steve had just finished the final calculations, and the first part of human experimentation was about to begin.

Dr Richard McFadden entered the final data into the computer.

After years of research and study, they were finally on the brink of publishing one of the most significant scientific breakthroughs since splitting the atom or discovering DNA.

Both men had been firm friends since meeting at the first-year fresher party some 22 years previous. They shared similar tastes and interests in women and music, comic books, and science.

They also shared an exuberance for the impossible, the farfetched, and the unreachable. Both longed to delve into scientific unknowns, way beyond the realms of mankind.

Both dreamed of the impossibility of time travel, and their fantasies had never waned... but balanced precariously on the edge of obsession.

The concept seemed fantastic. How could it be possible to move around in time? Actually, witness the past with your own eyes? Steve had been playing around with the notion of light-years and superlenses powerful enough to peer back through the universe, back through time.

But all his possibilities met with obstacles and the ridiculously unobtainable.

His initial ideas involved travelling faster than the speed of light to a solar system so far away it would still be receiving light waves emitted from earth many thousands of years ago. These, in turn, could be viewed through a super telescope. The theory sounded good – but the practicalities were beyond him.

He longed to disprove Einstein's Theory of Relativity. If only he could find a way for man to travel faster than the speed of light. But how? He didn't believe in the natural flow of time and space but felt useless in his pursuit to prove it.

Yet, since working with Richard, new and alternative ideas had started to flow, far from the traditional concepts of time travel.

Steve had majored in Physics, while Richard's studies focussed on Biochemistry with neurological behaviour and genetics as a sideline.

In his spare time, he was also an IT geek, which was invaluable to Steve.

It was really Richard's idea, but he was happy to share it with his bosom pal… and the awaiting glory that would surely follow their big breakthrough.

The idea was simple. What if a computer programme could read your memories? What if the data, the memories inside your brain, could be saved electronically to be replayed as video footage?

Richard had recently published a paper entitled 'Total Recall,' in-depth research on how the brain records and recalls information.

This thinking led to further developments. Neurones in the brain were merely electrical impulses. Thousands of neurones were located in the hippocampus, the part of the brain used to recall memory. Richard concluded that if he could find a way of externally harnessing these neurons, he would, at last, have the breakthrough they were looking for.

He discussed this at length with Steve, using two heads to calculate the more complex equations of his theory.

What if they could achieve the impossible? Find a way to visually record memories. What an archive that would leave for future generations!

It wouldn't be time travel perse, but travelling into the past through another memory – eyewitness accounts in real-time.

It is well known that conscious recall of memory accounts for a mere fraction of the data kept in the brain. If that were mined- the possibilities were endless – not to mention the ultimate biography of a life… every second caught on film.

The tricky part had been the connection between the brain and hardware. It would be perfect if Richard could link up a brain to a computer with a direct download facility. The theory sounded good, but how to convert the slideshow of life and transmit it from the brain to a computer screen?

Electrical activity in the brain is measured by a series of waves, Alpha, Beta, Delta, and Theta, all in differing amplitudes and frequencies. Suppose a computer programme could be written to convert these different frequencies to sound and light. In that case, it might just be possible…

The two worked on the idea for almost three years when the breakthrough happened late one night…

Richard had been developing a microchip to insert into the hippocampus area of the brain. Once inserted, this chip would send signals via wave frequencies, the same waves found in the brain.

These would lead to a receptor that would decode the wavelengths into sight and sound, similar to a radio transmitter or TV aerial. The receptor would be plugged into a computer hard drive, and the information streamed live onto the screen. It was an idea that should work in theory.

Steve procured two white rats from the science lab to test this. One died a few hours after the microchip had been inserted into its brain, but the other lived long enough to run the test several times. With the microchip successfully inserted into the rat's brain, they switched on the computer expectantly.

 At first, there was nothing. The rat sat in one corner of the cage, looking woeful with its tiny pink-shaven head. The screen was blank. Richard checked the wavelength meter. Although the rat looked inert and calm, the meter registered beta wavelengths, signifying mental activity. The wavelength frequencies were currently 15, but slowly the pointer started rising to 20 and then 30.

The limit for beta wavelengths is approximately 40 per second. The pointer wavered and swung round again, 35, then 40, 45, and 50. At this point, the rat let out a deafening screech, becoming suddenly frantic, running haphazardly up and down the cage. The computer screen crackled to life, black and white hazy lines appearing on the screen. The meter now registered 60 wavelengths per second as the rat ran around in circles in obvious distress, the whites of its eyes clearly showing.

Richard placed his hands over his ears to block out the piercing cries from the poor creature while Steve looked on in fascination, scanning the screen eagerly for the slightest image.

The rat began to foam at the mouth, a pink-tinged ghastly spume.

Unable to watch, Richard reached for a metal stand and brought it cleanly down onto the rat's head.

 The cries of pain stopped immediately, the poor rodent sprawled motionless on its side against the glass wall of the cage.

The pointer on the meter slowed and started to reverse down the scale, quickly moving from Beta to Delta, the wavelengths of deep and dreamless sleep, the frequency falling, 4, 3, 2,1, 0.

The rat was dead.

That evening had been a blow for the two scientists. They had come so far, so close, but the idea was yet to morph into a scientific breakthrough.

Richard studied his notes and records of observations made that night. He poured over them into the small hours, tired and drained of energy and sleep, his head full of theory and calculations, looking for a clue, some path... clarity.

It was during this time that the two scientists had their first quarrel. Both were fractious and irritable with the thought of failure. The usual optimism and camaraderie shifted uneasily into darker emotions. Steve, always jealous of his friends' ability, started to chide and goad Richard's ethical ways. After the incident with the rat, Richard had been reluctant to experiment further with live animals before they understood the failure of the first.

Steve wanted to try again immediately with more rats. *They were only vermin*, he said, and not worth the worry.

The usually generous Richard started to resent his colleague's lack of input into the research, realising he alone would make the eventual breakthrough.

One Friday evening, one week after the initial experiment, it all came to a head. Richard hadn't slept for nearly 48 hours, was at the end of his tether, and about to give up. Steve picked up on the subject of the rats once again, belittling his friend for letting ethics get in the way of progress. The final straw came. The usually mild-mannered Richard strode over and punched Steve straight in the stomach.

"When I stand up to receive the Nobel prize for science, it will be with a clear conscience."

Winded but not hurt by the blow, Steve staggered back to Richard.

"You? When YOU receive the prize, what about me? We agreed. This is a shared project, equal partnership. Equal merit?"

"It would be," snapped back Richard. If you'd contributed anything to the research. You're not interested in the work, only the glory. This is my project".

Squaring up to his attacker Steve looked as though he would return the punch and raised a fist towards his former pal. Instead, he lowered his arm and left the room, slamming the door on his way out.

Immediately the door closed, Richard regretted his actions. He slumped over the workbench, head in hands, wondering what to do next. His eyes closed, he could no longer think, and with his mind and body shutting down, he fell into a deep sleep.

. . .

Waking, Richard looked at his watch. He'd been out of it for almost ten hours. His neck ached from his slumped position, but his mind seemed incredibly calm. The magic of sleep had cleared and refreshed his overworked brain. He was ready to start again.

A thought suddenly struck him. Maybe the rat had been too stimulated? The trick was to clear and calm the mind before the experiment started. Perhaps not sleep, the recipient would need to be awake to stimulate the brain functioning, but what if the recipient's brainwaves could be slowed to delta frequency while still awake?

Several drugs were used during surgery to put patients into various levels of consciousness. If he were to adjust these slightly, they might suit his purpose.

But first, he had to make it up to Steve. He hadn't meant what he said. Steve had been with him from day one, and it was unthinkable that he would go on alone.

Flipping up his mobile, he pressed the quick dial button, the only number used for months, ready with his apologies and news.

Steve hadn't gone far. He'd spent the night in one of the beds reserved for the IVF patients in the genetics sector. He hadn't slept well, worrying that he'd lost his share in probably the most significant scientific breakthrough in decades. He was about to head for the hospital cafeteria for a strong coffee when his mobile started to bleep.

• • •

Having made up, the two men were soon back in the laboratory, working on a new anaesthetic that would immobilise the brain while leaving the individual conscious.

Richard, absorbed in his work, soon forgot the incident, while Steve both consciously and unconsciously continued to brood, keeping his feelings under control for the sake of the experiment.

Three weeks later, the serum containing the anaesthetic was ready. Long days and nights had passed, the two hardly speaking except over calculations and formulae. They were finally ready to test the serum.

Steve managed to smuggle a couple more laboratory white rats for the purpose. The experiment went well. Both rats were injected, and tests proved their brain activity decreased to low delta levels. The rats remained inert, yet their eyes were wide awake and watchful.

It was time to undertake the experiment again. Once anaesthetised, the rat was prepared. A tiny implant was injected into its brain, the receptor and computer switched on.

The computer screen was blank, bar a white, horizontal line. Richard wiped his brow. He was perspiring, his hands anxious in the moment. Clammy handed, he passed the receptor to Steve, standing relaxed yet intent, watching the screen through hard eyes.

Steve looked at the receptor and then at the rat lying inert in the corner of the glass cage, pink eyes watching him back in silence. His hand moved to the dial, turning up the frequency.

Nothing.

Steve's eyes blazed. He needed this experiment to work. Glancing at Richard, his hand moved again to the receptor, turning the dial to full frequency.

The eyes of the rat flickered. At the same time, the line on the screen began to take shape, the hazy fuzz of transmission filling the screen.

The rat's face began to twitch, whiskers bristling. Richard reached across to grab the receptor, fearing for the animal's safety, but Steve, catching his arm firmly, moved the receptor away. Taken aback by his friend's assertiveness, Richard conceded, eyes turned back to the screen.

The men watched silently, engrossed, the image flicking across their unblinking eyes, the screen now a haze of waves and lines, white specks and noise. It started, slowly, like some dismembered thing, the picture holding together, taking shape. Still in black and white, a foetal image, an outline, indistinct but definitely there.

They moved closer to the screen, silent and open-mouthed. On the screen before them was the picture of a giant white rat, probably the mother of the lab rat – its first memories. The lines and haze began to shift as they watched, forming patterns, ghostly shapes, white against the black background, as a low hum vibrated through the air. Muffled squeaks boomed through the speakers. Before breaking up, the picture lasted for a few moments, returning to grey lines and distortion.

It didn't seem much, but it was everything. The experiment had been a success.

Steve broke the silence, raising his hands and punching the air. He walked across and shook his friend excitedly by the shoulders.

Richard raised his head, "And the rat is still alive," he smiled back.

For the next few weeks, they continued to experiment, changing the dose of anaesthetic and the frequency of the receptor until the results were clear and consistent. The pictures and sounds received were nearly all the same. The life of a lab rat was typically unvaried and mundane, but at least it proved the theory.

Richard was ready to announce the breakthrough, but Steve held back. What if they could publish their findings with human results?

Richard was dubious. They'd only been testing rats for a couple of weeks, and look what had happened to the first rat!

But Steve was persistent. No rats had died during the last few weeks, and besides, look how more credible their research would be with human results. Steve calculated that the experiment would work if they multiplied the serum dosage by the man to rat weight ratio.

Although reluctant, Richard was eager to test the research on the human brain. Steve faltered; the only drawback would be the lack of volunteers.

"I'll do it," spoke Rich solemnly, "it's my experiment. We'll try it tomorrow".

· · ·

The following morning was clear and bright. Dr Richard McFadden rose early to watch the dawn. He had not slept well; both fear and excitement had resulted in vivid dreams of his father calling to him as a child, but he could not hear and had been pursued by a giant white rat, eyes red and shining. He'd woken suddenly with a start, just as the rat had caught up with him.

Slipping on his jeans and T-shirt, he headed for the laboratory.

When Richard arrived, Dr Steven Wilson was already in the room, wearing his white coat and mixing liquids in a beaker. He'd prepared the serum and wanted to get started before his friend could change his mind.

Richard glanced at the apparatus ready for him, the serum, hypodermic needles, the microscopic implant suspended in saline solution.

He held out his hand.

"To the present, the past, and future, my friend."

Sitting, Richard rolled up his sleeve, his face fixed with anxiety.

Steve strapped him into the chair. Once the serum started to work, his body would become flaccid. He made the final preparations in silence, the atmosphere tight and formal. Squeezing the hypodermic to release excess fluid, the men looked each other steadily in the eye.

"Ready?"

Richard nodded, and Steve started to administer the serum. It was fast-acting, and within two minutes, he slumped forward in the chair, kept upright only by the restraining straps. His eyes remained open and watchful.

Steve loaded the implant into a needle 8 inches in length, long enough to inject the implant through the back of the eye socket and up into the brain's cortex. The serum acted as an anaesthetic, and Richard didn't feel a thing but gazed into his friend's face as he carried out the procedure.

It took more than half an hour. The membrane surrounding the brain was tough and resistant. Steve had to apply slow pressure to push the needle through the layers of sinew and into position. With shaking hands, he put down the needle; the first part of the experiment was complete. Richard remained slumped in the chair, but his eyes were bright and alert.

Steve powered up the hardware by connecting the frequency monitor and receptor to the computer. They were ready to go.

Nothing happened at first. The computer monitor stayed silent and blank. Steve reached for the receptor and turned the dial. Richard's eyes flickered. Still nothing. Steve turned up the frequency.

And then it began. At first, the wavy lines and hazy shapes appeared, with a lot of noise and fuzz.

Eventually, the dim outline of a face started to form. Richard's eyes flickered towards the screen as his father's image appeared, and then his mother's - young and smiling. More faces took shape, friends, relatives, a jumble of images, old and new memories flooding the screen.

Holidays and birthdays, football in the park, girlfriends all zipped past in a whirl of light and sound. Richard's eyes flickered from right to left, rapid eye movements while still awake.

The frequency monitor showed the brainwaves shift from Delta to Beta, accelerating to over 50 a second. Steve checked Richard's vital signs. His heart was racing, and his blood pressure high, but he was fit and looked ok. Besides, the experiment had to run its course.

The images continued to flood the monitor, some so quickly that the pictures could scarcely be seen. Steve turned down the sound, a gabble of voices and noise from the past filling the air, bearing down on him until he could no longer bear it.

The download continued for several hours. Steve checked Richard every 10 minutes until the images finally slowed and the screen froze. The last picture was of Steve standing before him in the laboratory.

Richard's eyes relaxed until he was staring at the screen. His breathing was regular, and his heart rate and blood pressure normal.

Steve smiled at his friend and kissed him lightly on the forehead. Richard watched blankly as his friend reached over to the computer and, raising a hand, reached over to the keyboard and pressed the delete key.

Richard's eyes widened in horror as, one by one, the images flicked back across the screen faster than before, disappearing into the ether, never to be seen again. His whole life deleting before his very eyes.

Steve glanced at the monitor. The brainwaves were now changing from Alpha to Beta before finally settling at Delta, the frequency lessening with each second.

Richard looked at Steve, struggling to hold onto the moment, as his old friend glanced back, a look of triumph burning coldly in his bright eyes.

The brain waves slowed. Steve counted down, 5, 4,3,2,1..... Zero.

Oblivion.

The End

Inspired by a cocktail pianist on a cruise with mum.

Nosfortissimo

The notes sailed overhead. Each one a wave crashing above, beyond, and below, leaving her insignificant, floating, a trail of white foam on a billowing ocean. Submerged and drowning.

He sat in the shabby splendour of a former era, wearing the passage of time, a cloak wrapped around him, all darkness and shade. His features were set from a forgotten period, angular and distinct.

She could see the pianist's hands, sweeping the notes lightly with a deft elegance, feeling each touch of his fingers along her spine, pressing softly into her skin. Shivering, she allowed the storm to pass through her.

She'd stumbled into the bar by accident- if life is chance and not governed by some unforeseen guiding hand.

The bar had been dark enough to match her mood and far enough from her usual haunts not to be disturbed. Candles set in red glass jars bled the only light into the room, tiny hearts flickering in the darkness.

She wanted to sit alone with only her thoughts for company. A drink and the darkness were enough. She was not prepared for the music. When closing her eyes, the gentle rhythm rose above the low hum of voices. Softly at first, lulling, stirring the brooding emotions within, dangerous and dark.

The spell was cast. Time and space became nothing. All was music. And she was part of the melody, spiralling and billowing in its magnificent sails.

The pianist peered out into the room before him and away to the distance. The room was dark, with the occasional lamp casting a grotesque red glow onto the blank faces before him.

He had been here for all eternity, every bar the same, more or less. The people changed, yet all carried the same tired, indifferent expressions. The puffed-up, blousey faces of women well past their prime, the shadows making carnival masks of their over rouged cheeks and heavily lipsticked mouths. Stained, gloved hands grasping at the stems of tiny glasses filled with coloured liquids dripping endlessly down their flabby jewelled throats.

The men fared no better. Slicked back greasy hair, eyes rheumy with self-indulgence, jaws set with the bitterness of life. Fingers pulpy around cut-glass beakers of whisky and gin.

He despised them all.

Yet, he played for them. Night after night. Soulful and beautiful melodies, but he did not touch or stir the crowd. Their hearts were as hard as the lines on their faces. So too, the pianist detached. His trained fingers played with a technical brilliance that was not part of him.

But tonight, something was different. He could taste it in the air the moment he started to play and felt it in the darkness of his soul. He played the usual repertoire, his fingers slipping naturally along the chords and notes. Black to white, adagissimo to allegrissimo without a thought. And yet, tonight, it was his own heart that beat out the rhythm.

She opened her eyes. The pianist seemed to be looking in her direction. His serious face looked away, down at his hands running over the keyboard, then over his left shoulder as if searching for someone or something but never finding. His hair was dark, his eyes brooding over the piano across the darkness.

Somehow she felt empathy towards him. Her mood and emotions were fragile, the music touching something within as if he played only for her. How to engage, how to distract those searching eyes? She caught his gaze at last and smiled shyly.

The pianist noticed the new face. He often looked into the crowd but barely took notice. Suddenly she was there with eyes looking at him. And then she smiled, and by some natural chemistry, he did something he rarely did, he smiled back.

His whole demeanour changed, she noticed, as he smiled. A boyish youthfulness transformed him from a dark creature to an angel of light. His smile became one with the music, and she was lost.

He rarely smiled, and the sensation felt foreign. So alien that the very act of smiling made him smile again. He looked down at his fingers playing mechanically without him, masking the emotions forming behind his eyes. He had been alone for some time now. The women in his life had been few. He loved quickly, passionately, but the objects of his affection barely lasted through the first movement.

Even the job suited him, the twilight hours, the late shift heading slowly towards morning. Nature reflecting man.

But tonight. This seemed different. Why did he feel so compelled to her, a stranger? It wasn't a mere physical attraction, although what he could see in the gloom was pleasing. A fresh face, light eyes, and a graceful and slender pale neck, the pulse of life gently beating within.

 A bead of sweat formed on his upper lip, and a coolness crossed his brow. Could this be different? Could this be the one? His eyes once again moved to his fingers, and this time he played from deep within his soul. His fingers, light and swift tripped and caressed the keys like never before, the music sweet and hypnotic until all was lost in the melody.

Even the regulars noticed. They shifted in their seats, lifting their heavy lids towards the pianist, breaking off their sullied and stilted conversations to listen.

The pianist glanced at his watch. 2am. His time was approaching.

Glancing towards the bar, he caught the attention of a waiter. He would send over a drink by way of an introduction. Something sophisticated, a martini cocktail, perhaps?

He smiled, a plan forming in the shadows. The night would be his again, the master of darkness. Only four hours until dawn, until it was time to shut away from the daylight, the living. Time enough to release the demon within, taste the essence of life itself.

He would drink to that.

The woman was surprised yet found it inwardly pleasing when the waiter handed her the cocktail, indicating the pianist. She raised her glass. First to the pianist in acknowledgement, then to her lips, eyes shining, drinking to life.

And thus sealing her fate.

The End

I often think of the ending to a story before I even know what the story will entail. This is a perfect example. I was obsessed with the ending. Possibly, I will make this into a longer piece at some point, but I had to get it out of my head! Written during the hot summer of COVID lockdown.

Resurrection

It was mid-June, and the night was humid. The sky bruised a deep purple, only one shade away from darkness.

She couldn't sleep, the air thick and sticky, hair plastered to the nape of her neck, and the confines of the bed as airless as a tomb.

But it wasn't the heat that kept her awake.

A million thoughts held her back from the comfort of sleep, ratcheting through her mind on constant replay.

Throwing back the duvet, she stepped across the wooden floor – and as she did, caught sight of her naked self in the cheval mirror that had once belonged to her grandmother.

The vision made her heart race – white skin eerily reflected in the moonlight – her mother's face – not her own- looking back.

'Mother' – the word slipped out before she could catch it – disappearing into the gloom.

Of course, it was not her mother but her own face, now lined with age. When had she grown so old?

Stepping to the open window- she stared into the night – her troubles too heavy to see the beauty before her.

Life has been a waste – she thought. I am middle-aged and have allowed life to pass me by. Soon I shall be dead, and there will be nothing to show for it.

It was a wallowing – self-pity that weighed her down – preventing her from moving forward – from getting on with life.
She had spent the last five years looking after her mother – watched the slow descent into senility.

Yet her mother had been strong and raged against the dying of the light – and even when robbed of both faculties and memory – her spirit remained.

Her mother had been a fighter, "*I don't want to die*" – she had cried out as the world around her became unrecognisable – even her own daughter.

Then, in the end – she had left the world quietly, with dignity – leaving a wordless, gaping gash that would never heal.

The grief had been too much – it had consumed her. The love for her mother was too great. Every ounce of love used up until her heart was a desert.

And when love is gone – what remains?

It was then that the world began to close around her.

The woman closed her eyes against the gathering grief, the thud, thudding of life making her dizzy.

How much longer could she go on like this? There was no one close – no children. She never wanted anyone to feel such grief for her – the responsibility outweighed any joy a family might bring.

Just her.

It seemed natural to get dressed – even though it was the middle of the night as if some unseen hand guided her. Without thinking, she pulled on her old tracksuit bottoms and a t-shirt, stuffing her bare feet into a battered pair of Birkenstock's. Her hair was a mess, tousled with sleep and sweat, but what did it matter… nothing mattered in the end.

Although warm, the air was fresher as she stepped out into the night, quietly closing the door behind her. The back lane was overgrown, and the air heavy with the scent of roses. The pale pink blooms cast white against the dark hedgerow made her pause.

The sweet air enveloped her as she stood, unmoving in the moonlight. In her grief, she had not expected this, and the moment came upon her suddenly like a lover's kiss – fragile and tender.

Closing her eyes against the night, she could feel her body sway as though drunk on the sweet perfume. A strange vibration filled her- was all around her – and somehow, she knew the universe was calling out to her. It was then that she felt it… a heady sense of eternity.

Everything that had ever been or ever would be was around her as one energy, and suddenly she felt part of the great flow.

Opening her eyes, she looked to the heavens, and suddenly she could see the whole of humanity – right there in the stars. She had tasted the incomprehensible meaning of life, and suddenly it all made sense.

With a sudden fervour, she set off down the path, sure of what she must do.

It wasn't far.

Already she could hear the river, the endless stream making its way toward the sea. Soon she was on the bridge, the water alive and far below- whispering secrets that only she could hear.

It all made sense now. It was so simple. She smiled and pulled the t-shirt over her head, kicking off the sandals and tracksuit bottoms until she was naked.

The slight breeze over the bridge was deliciously cooling, and she held her arms wide as she stood on the edge.

The coldness of the water was a welcome release as she plunged into the depths - her shocked heart pumping furiously –

Live… live… live!

The End

One of my favourite books growing up was 'The Goalkeeper's Revenge' By Bill Naughton. Good, honest storytelling – often thought-provoking. This is my humble attempt in that style…

The Chicken Whisperer

Chicken George was a special lad who lived at the end of our street. My mother said he had 'Down's Syndrome, but it didn't mean a lot to us kids. We just thought he was a bit unusual.

Of course, he looked a bit different and didn't talk that much, but that didn't bother us. He was just one of the gang.

His mother, a worried-looking woman, treated him like a baby, used to make him wrap up all year long, even in summer, and we had some hot 'uns back then. But Chicken George didn't mind. He'd wait until his mother was out of sight and strip off down to his vest like the rest of us.

It wasn't just his condition that made him unique, though. He had a natural affinity with nature.

George had a gentle soul, and it was as if the birds and small living creatures could sense that and formed a special bond with him. He could feed wild birds out of his hand and always seemed to be nursing a sick creature. From a blackbird with a broken wing to a fledgeling sparrow fallen from its nest, you name it, he would take care of it.

Mr Stevenson had a large square allotment and grew every vegetable you could think of. He also kept chickens, twenty noisy brown hens that supplied most of the street with their weekly egg ration. Then one summer, they stopped laying, just like that. One lad said he'd seen a fox prowling around, which had probably scared them, so Mr Stevenson secured the chicken run until it was more like Fort Knox, but still, the hens refused to lay.

One day as we lads walked past the allotments, Mr Stevenson called out jokingly to George to *have a word* with his *girls*.

Before we could stop him, George took the man at his word and hopped over the hedge and into the chicken coop.

It was a sight to behold. George sat amongst the chicken shit and peelings, arms outstretched towards the birds and making clucking noises.

We shouted at him to come away, not to be so soft, and that his Mam would be after him for ruining his britches, but he ignored us and concentrated on the hens.

And do you know, after a few minutes, the chickens came up to him. Soon he was picking them up, gently stroking their feathers and speaking softly.

Well, we lads just stood there in amazement. We knew George was special, but we hadn't seen anything like that.
After attending to all twenty birds, George hopped back over the hedge and smiled.

'What you been saying to them chickens, George?' we asked good-humouredly

George just looked back at us with a wide grin and winked.

A couple of days later, we were walking past the allotment when Mr Stevenson shouted to us, all excited like.

'George,' he shouted, 'Av got sommat' for you lad. My girls have started layin' again, I don't know what you said to 'em, but it's worked wonders".

George all smiles - pushed to the front of the group, where Mr Stevenson pressed 2 bob into his hand.

'I reckon if you come and look in on my girls a few days a week, there'll be a few more bob coming your way, George. Take these for your Mam", and with that, he handed George a box of the biggest and brownest eggs we'd ever seen.

And every day after that, George would spend half an hour amongst the chickens. His mother made him wear his old clothes, but she was glad of the extra eggs and money.

And from that day on, we called him 'Chicken George.'

Happy days.

It was only as we grew older that the differences really began to show. As we matured into young men, George was left behind. We finished school and started work and courting, walking into a world where he couldn't follow, not in those days anyway.
I still used to see him around on my way home from work from time to time. He'd be skulking around the streets or going to the shop for his Mam.
He was no longer carefree, his old playmates had deserted him, and he was locked in a place where he was neither boy nor man. He spent the days on the dreary, grey streets, pacing up and down like a caged animal, full of frustration and neglect. His once happy, open face developed an old man's scowl. Even his clothes looked shabby, and his mother, now a widow, could ill afford new clothes for a son that was permanently wanting.

It was a sad state, yet when he saw me, his face would light up, and I saw a glimmer of the old George. He would give me the thumbs-up, and I'd smile and do the same before hurrying back home to get ready for a night out with the boys.

As he got older, George became a bit of a handful. I heard it mostly from my mother, but I had the chance to see it just once for myself.

He was on the High Street with his Mam, something had upset him, and he was flying into a rage, kicking and screaming, legs and arms shooting out wildly as if he was having a fit. Although still a boy in his ways, George had the body of a strong man and knocked over the neatly stacked boxes outside the greengrocers - apples and oranges bouncing down the street and into the gutters.

His mother just stood, looking old and worn in a shabby coat and hat.

She caught my eye, and I hurried quickly past, not knowing what to say, feeling guilty about something though not quite sure what.

I only saw George once after that. Typically it was as I passed the old allotments. Mr Stevenson still kept his chickens, and George looked after them - sat amongst the shit and scrapings and bits of feathers, whispering to the birds.

He didn't see me or pretended not to. Our worlds were so different now. I wanted to call out and say 'Hi,' but something inside me made me feel ashamed, and I turned away.

It was a couple of years later after I'd got married and moved away from home, that I heard the news.

George had been taken away to an institution. Apparently, he'd become violent, and his mother couldn't cope. It was one afternoon that sealed his fate. George had gone into the chicken coop as usual and, without warning, had killed them all. Just like that, George had wrung the scrawny necks of his beloved hens.

Mr Stevenson had found him weeping, sat among the shit and the feathers and the blood, the mangled bodies of the birds all around him.

The End

As a child, I always seemed to be gazing into the horizon – onto a sunny hilltop far away and wishing I was there. I suppose my inspiration comes from those memories…

Distant Horizons

As a child, Simba had been a dreamer. There had been little else to do in his small, poor village. Even dreams were a luxury that he had to fit in between daily chores.

His mother would often catch him leaning against the fence with his eyes closed, face towards the sun, and lost in his own world when he should have been feeding the chickens or sweeping the yard.

He was often at the receiving end of her sharp words or hand. His mother was not a cruel woman, but life had made her hard. She looked older than her years, poverty eating away at her youth, eroding the vitality and light which had once made her the finest looking girl in the village.

Simba did not go to school but spent all day working on the small farm for his mother. At just nine years old, he was the man of the household since his father had died many years passed.

His favourite time of the day was the late afternoon. Having completed most of his daily tasks, he would walk a little way from his homestead. He would follow the river that babbled away to the west, following the path of the sun to where it would finally rest over the distant mountains.

Simba's eyes would trace the river's winding path, glistening through the open countryside. They would take in the yellowing fields of dry grass, the patches of green vegetation, the shadows and shades of lone trees, wiry dark shadows amongst the flat landscape. His gaze lifted higher and higher with the rise of the land until finally, they rested on the purple and grey hills in the distance.

To Simba, the mountains seemed a magical place, rising magnificently above everyone and everything for miles around. Sometimes in the winter months, he could see the patches of white snow clinging to the tall peaks and in the ravines and gullies - glistening in the afternoon sun.

His heart ached peculiarly whenever he looked at the mountains. A low, dull sensation in his breast made him feel happy yet sad. A deep yearning for something he did not understand.

No one in his village had been to the mountains, no one knew how far away the mountains were, and they seemed an impossible distance, especially to a young boy.

He'd heard stories told by the elders of the mountain regions, dark tales of strange tribes and monsters, the likes of which made the hairs on the back of his neck quiver.

Yet, these images did not lessen his growing love for the mountains. They intrigued him and tugged at his mind, awakening his curiosity and leaving him wanting.

The years passed quickly by, Simba's days following the same pattern. He kept up his daily vigil, staring at the mountains, lost in their beauty and always dreaming of the future, his eyes glued to the horizon.

When Simba was 18, his mother died, and he was left alone in the world. He was tired of the small village, living with the same people he had grown up with, and yearned for travel and adventure. With no one left to depend on him, the possibilities, although limited, started to open up.

One evening, the mountains looked particularly beautiful. The mauves and lavenders of the heavens merged with the greys and purples of the hills, and the summits glinted in the golden glory of the late afternoon sun. He made a plan. He would travel to the mountains, and he would follow his heart.

There was quite a buzz within the village as Simba prepared for his journey. He sold off the hut where he and his mother had lived, selling the few chickens, goats, and pigs. In fact, he sold everything he and his mother had owned or swapped them for the essentials he would need for such a journey.

He bought a horse and supplies, with just a little extra money leftover should he need it.
The night before he left, the village elder called Simba into his hut. He had a special gift, a tribal band to wear around his neck. The elder placed it over Simba's head. It was a unique band, bearing sacred tribal symbols to keep him safe from harm until he returned home. Simba thanked the elder, secretly thinking that he would never return once he left.

The whole village turned out to see Simba set off. There was music and dancing, kisses and hugs for Simba, the man, the adventurer. The village girls dressed in their brightest clothes and fussed over him. They had never really paid much attention to the quiet dreamer they'd all made fun of as children. But now, the girls jostled each other for Simba's attention. Each had a glint in their eye and a soft word for the young man.

'Remember me, Simba,' 'Come back and marry me, Simba,' they called, laughing and teasing.

Simba was taken aback, flattered by this newfound attention, but he gazed at the mountains to the west, his one true desire. He felt the dull ache once again within his breast and, waving goodbye for the last time, set off astride his horse. Now he would finally leave the boy behind.

It was a beautiful sunny day as he set off. He didn't have a map but would follow the river's path, keeping the mountains in his sight.

The morning turned into a blisteringly hot afternoon, and Simba had to rest by a grove of trees.

He ate part of the bread and cheese he'd brought with him and fell asleep in the sun.

When he awoke, the sun was setting over the beautiful mountains, and as the sun disappeared, the air became chill. Simba hadn't expected the cold; he had no warm hut to lie down in, so he huddled beneath the horse blanket and dreamt of the mountains beneath the stars.

He didn't sleep well, the ground below was hard, and he was cold, but soon the sun was up again, and glancing at his beloved mountains once more, Simba smiled and, mounting his horse set off to the west.

This carried on for several days, Simba waking early and travelling in the relative coolness of the morning until the heat proved too much for him. He shivered alone beneath the stars at night, the mountains forever watchful, always beautiful, rising higher and higher as he approached.

For ten days and ten nights, Simba rode across the land through barren, parched fields, the vegetation scrubby and harsh, providing little refuge. Weary from the travelling and lack of sleep, he found he was running low on provisions, and hunger pangs added to his discomfort.

By the tenth night, Simba had almost reached the base of the mountains. In the dimming light, the dark mass of rock loomed above him. As he stood in their shadow, he shivered. The once beautiful mountains now seemed menacing in the darkness. But he had made it here, his dream. He would rest easily now, and all would be well in the morning.

For once, Simba slept well, yet his sleep was full of dreams: of home, young girls waving to him, friends laughing and joking, his mother young again and calling to him.

The day broke cloudless and bright. Yet now he was here, Simba felt a little disappointed. Up close, the mountains did not look so beautiful or mysterious. They rose above him, brutal and bleak. The mountain paths looked steep, but he found one the horse could manage, and they set off up the slope together.

Simba's heart weighed heavy as the weary pair started their ascent. After a couple of hours, the horse needed resting, and dismounting, he sat on a flat rock.

He reached into his knapsack and pulled out the remains of his provisions, a piece of hard mouldy bread, and a scant wedge of cheese.

Slowly nibbling at the meagre breakfast, he gazed from the mountains across the land spread out below him. His eyes followed the river back to its source, back along the miles and miles he had travelled, where the sun's rays filtered softly down into a slight hollow in the distance, the valley containing his village.

Simba felt a peculiar yet familiar dull ache within his breast and wondered why.

The End

I actually visited a travelling Freak Show as described in the story while taking a holiday in Cornwall in the 1980s. I wonder if it still exists? A great inspiration for a story.

Freak Show

Something stirred his memory. Perhaps it was the move – sorting out the forgotten detritus of life. It almost seemed unreal, and he wondered whether it had been a dream – a boyish flight of fancy – but he'd never been that type of lad.

But now, moving back to the place of his childhood, something played on his conscience. Maybe it was growing old, but something didn't sit easy. All his life, he'd been independent, with no wife, no children. His career had been everything. Now, ill health forced him into sheltered accommodation, and for the first time in his life, he reflected on the past.

School day reminders hidden in an old biscuit tin had been buried away at the back of a cupboard for more than 60 years, and even though the contents belonged to him, he had difficulty finding affinity with the objects within.

With a trembling hand, he lifted out an old black & white photograph of his school days. Three rows of fresh-faced young men smiled back at him. Where were they now? he wondered. Faces he hadn't seen in decades. Either dead or infirm, he thought without self-pity.

He even remembered some of the names, Joe White, Henry Perkins, and little Arthur Jones, nicknamed *shrimp* because of his size. They'd been good lads, but he couldn't remember any of them being particular friends.

He was about to put back the lid, shut away the memories when something at the bottom of the tin caught his eye. A small silver bell attached to a ribbon.

He'd forgotten all about that until now. A twinge in his heart made him pause for a moment. It had all been such a very long time ago…

Alan was 10 years old. Well, 10 and a half, to be exact, if you were counting the months and days, which Alan did. He had a large calendar on his bedroom wall that his father had bought home from the office, and he ticked off the days with a thick black pencil, counting down the weeks until he would be 11 and nearly a man

There were exactly 6 months and 12 days to his 11th birthday. It couldn't come soon enough.

It did seem a long way off, though. It was the middle of the summer holidays, and July stretched ahead of him, a chain of sunny days lining up like the segments of a railway track, each one identical.

You would have thought a boy aged 10 would have been thoroughly content. He was on holiday, the sun was shining, but Alan was bored. He was the kind of child that could not amuse himself. Nature didn't intrigue him like other boys. He didn't collect worms or beetles, fish in ponds, or scurry through the countryside looking for berries or mushrooms or anything boys usually do.

He didn't swim in the river, kick a football, or play tennis but spent most of the holiday skulking about, hands in pockets kicking at stones, and being generally disagreeable.

Alan had been away at boarding school during term time and didn't know many boys from the village. He lived with his parents on the outskirts of a small hamlet and didn't mix with the locals. Then again, he didn't really want to. All the other boys wanted to play football or cricket, and he wasn't that keen. He wasn't bothered about much apart from growing into a man. Then he was sure the world and all its wonders would be his.

On one sweltering afternoon, Alan's mother called him from the house. She wanted him to run an errand in the village. Alan kicked at a tree. He had nothing to do, was fed up, but would rather stand and do nothing than go into the village. His mother was insistent and called to him again in her no-nonsense voice, so he knew not to argue.

It was only a 10-minute walk, but he dawdled along the lane, looking out across the fields. The sun was at its highest, and Alan was hot. He dragged his feet in the dust, and the 10-minute walk took half an hour.

The village was quaint, as old English villages often are, or at least were in the years before the war. There was a small post office, one shop, and a butcher and baker's van came twice a week. At the centre stood a small red-bricked school where most village children learned to read and write but very little else, yet adequate enough for the opportunities awaiting them.

But Alan was different. His father worked in the City, in business, where Alan would go someday. These thoughts made him feel superior, and he held his head high as he passed a group of boys kicking around a football in the street. They smiled and waved at Alan, recognising him, for they were good-natured children with kind hearts and no malice. He nodded and put his head down. That was something his father would do.

Arriving at the shop, the bell tinkled as he entered. The old lady behind the counter smiled generously at Alan, recognising him from the big house. Alan handed over the shopping list his mother had made, he didn't like small talk, but he didn't want to appear rude. He started choosing some sweets.

"Will you be going to the Fair, young Master Alan," the shopkeeper inquired.

Alan kept his eyes on the sweets and mumbled that he didn't know anything about it.

"There's a poster here, and it looks fun. A young lad like you should have some fun", she carried on with a gleam in her eye.

Alan didn't want to appear impolite; he had the family reputation to think of, so he glanced up. The old woman was pointing to a poster on the wall. Alan read, showing little interest. A large printed paper in gay colours and exotic writing heralded the arrival of a fair coming to the Village Green in two days.

There would be horses and rides, toffee apples, illusions, games, and all sorts of wonders and marvels. At the very bottom of the poster, bold letters announced the attraction of 'A Glorious Freak Show.' Dr V. Mysterious would present his collection of the strange and wonderful, collected from across the globe. The show promised curiosities that had never been seen before, sights that were both horrifying and terrible, marvellous and exotic.

Alan's mouth turned up a little at the edges in scorn. Although only young, he had adopted a look of disdain from his father. It was what a man would do. He had never heard of anything so ridiculous, and he told the old woman so.

"It's probably a lot of trickery," Alan indicated the final item on the poster. "A fool and his money are soon parted. My father always says that". Alan tried to sound superior.

Surprised at such a serious and sour-faced young man, the old lady laughed.

"You're very cynical for one so young," she smiled back at the strange lad.

"My father says I have an old head on young shoulders. I will go into business soon".

The old woman teased him. "You won't be wanting those sweets then if you're a city gent, eh?"

Alan stood red-faced and in a dilemma. He wanted the sweets badly but didn't want to lose face.

"No, I will just have what is on Mother's list," With that, the boy turned his back on the old woman.

Outside, he saw the boys who called him to play and kicked a football over to where he was walking.

Feeling decidedly hot-tempered and irritable, Alan kicked the ball back hard, so hard it hit the corner of a curb and burst.

The boys cried out in dismay. They didn't have another ball. Alan couldn't care less and set off running back home.

He gave no thought to the fair again until the night before it arrived. His mother asked him if he would take along another young boy, the son of a friend visiting for the weekend.

Alan scowled. The young boy was only seven, he didn't want to babysit, and anyway, he didn't want to go to the silly fair.

But his mother insisted.

The day came bright and clear and hot. Arthur, the young boy, was wearing a sailor suit and looked ridiculous and a lot younger than his years. The two boys set off, the younger full of excitement and glee, the older walking hands in pockets, slouching like an old man against the sunshine.

They could hear the fair before they arrived, carnival music, the sounds of animals, and loud voices calling out to come and buy. Turning the corner, the sight was remarkable, trailers, horses, canvas tents, and every colour imaginable. Everything was bright and gaudy. Even the people were colourful, wearing exotic costumes and dazzling jewellery.

The two boys walked past the stalls, Alan with an air of contempt, young Arthur delighted by all he saw. There were toffee apples and candy floss, hook a duck, and games of chance. In the centre of the field gleamed a steam carousel with beautiful plumed horses travelling up and down. Round and round, they danced, their painted faces regal and proud. Men on stilts, jugglers and unicyclists, a dancing bear cub, and men on horses jostled through the crowds.

Arthur wanted to go on the carousel. He chose a beautiful white mount with a red mane and waved eagerly to Alan as he circled around and around.

Alan was bored. The ride would last a few minutes; he would have a walk to pass the time.

A large and antiquated canvas tent was erected on the very edge of the green. Outside, an old painted sign displayed in bold type 'Dr V Mysterious Famous Freak Show Admittance 1 shilling' in peeling letters.

Alan felt his lip curl slightly. What rubbish. He was about to turn back to the colour and light when a voice called out to him.

"Young Sir, will you not step inside the world of Dr Mysterious?"

Alan looked around. Stepping out of the tent was an old man, dressed from top to toe in black, a relic from another era. He wore a pointed beard, and although his face was old, his eyes were unnaturally young and vibrant. Around his neck, Alan noticed he wore a tiny silver bell attached to a black velvet ribbon that jangled slightly as he walked.

The man held out a thin, wiry arm to Alan, beckoning him closer. He was set to walk away when the man called again, his voice light and reedy.

"Why don't you step inside, Alan?"

The lad spun around. "But how do you know my na...", but the old man had already disappeared inside.

Alan was intrigued. He looked around him; the carousel was still turning and would continue for several minutes. He made his way to the tent and peered behind the canvas.

It was very dark, and Alan squinted to focus, stepping further inside.

A musty cavernous smell made him cough and then sneeze. He looked around. There were rows upon rows of old shelves, and it looked more like a junk shop than a Freak Show. Old bottles and jars were muddled together in a seemingly haphazard fashion.

Alan approached one of the shelves. It contained a series of dark, murky bottles covered in years of cobwebs and dust. Each one appeared to be filled with liquid, and there were strange objects, unidentifiable lumps immersed in the grimy depths.

Each jar wore an old faded label written in inky, spindly writing. Alan could hardly make out the words, so spidery and scrawled were the letters. He looked closer, mouthing the words.

"Two-headed …something", Alan scratched his head.

"Two-headed lamb foetus," came a strange shrill voice behind him.

It made Alan jump, and he turned around quickly to find the old man in black right behind him. The man looked older than on first impression. Up close, his skin had a yellowing papery texture, like the labels on the old jars and bottles. His teeth were yellow too, his eyes rheumy, pale and silver, and shining in the dark.

"Here, take a look," the man called in his piping voice, handing a dusty bottle to the boy.

Alan clutched at the bottle delicately; it seemed so old and fragile. The top was black, sealed with an ancient cork and sealing wax. The glass was deep green in colour, the contents cloudy, murky; it was like the pond back home. Alan swirled the jar around to get a better look.

"Careful," cried the man sharply, "that is very old and rare."

Alan stared at the bottle; he could see something, in the shape of a giant tadpole, with two lumps sticking out of the top. It looked old and unsavoury. Disgusted, Alan handed the bottle back to the old man, clearly unimpressed.

"You are not easily pleased-I can see that," observed the man. "Let me show you some of the other exhibits."

The man took Alan by the arm and led him past the unusual collection of dull coloured jars and unrecognizable contents. These contained an unborn baby with withered legs, a lamb born inside out, and the foetus of conjoined twins, all legs and arms twisting and turning in their foul suspension.

To Alan, they looked like lumps of meat or dead animals. He'd already dismissed the ghoulish wonders as fakes, objects made by the old man himself to fool the paying public.

Alan gave his queer sour look to the old man

"Now, my friend," the man hissed into Alan's ear, "The show is over. That will be one shilling".

Alan looked at the man. One shilling, this wasn't worth one penny.

"Hmm," said the old man understanding the sour look. "You don't want to give me a shilling. You're not impressed, eh?" Maybe you can give me something else in exchange? Tell me, if you had one wish, what would it be?

Alan thought for a moment. He thought of toys and books the other boys had. He wasn't really interested in those things. Then a thought struck him. "I want to be a man, like my father."

The old man smiled wisely. "In time, my young friend, in time. I can grant you your wish, but you must give me something in return, something you can easily do without, something you won't even notice?"

The man thought for a while, then went behind a small table and brought out an amethyst-colored bottle, gleaming brightly amongst the old and the dusty.

"If you blow into this bottle, we can forget about the shilling. And your wish will become true…surely that's a bargain?"

Alan looked cautiously at the man and then the bottle. The man must be crazy? But, what would it hurt blowing into a bottle, and he would still have his shilling left to spend on candy floss and ice cream.

"Don't worry, my friend, you are only giving me something you no longer need. You want to be a man, don't you?" the old man smiled.

Alan shrugged and took the bottle. What harm could there be – the man was obviously a crank. Wiping the rim with his sleeve, he prepared to breathe into the bottle.

"Slowly, slowly, a nice deep breath, fill the bottle." The man's eyes glimmered as Alan pursed his lips.

He blew into the bottle until he had no breath left, the little man clapping with glee as he finished, quickly snatching away the bottle and putting a large cork stopper into the top to seal it.

The man must be crazy, thought Alan, suddenly feeling quite nervous and wanting to leave the tent.

"Wait a moment," called the man in black as Alan turned to leave.

"Your wish, I need to grant you your wish, to become a man. Come here."

Alan looked at the man. What if he was crazy? Well, he looked frail, and Alan could run fast.

The boy walked up to where the man stood. Placing an old gnarled hand on the young shoulder, the elder looked the boy full in the face, the silver eyes glinting catlike in the dark.

Taking hold of the little bell and ribbon, he removed it from around his neck and placed it over Alan's head. The bell gave out a shrill tinkling sound as it dangled from the black ribbon. . With that, the man moved back into the rear of the tent, disappearing into the shadows.

Alan shivered. Was that it? He wondered if the man was coming back? It was cold and gloomy, and he wanted light. Besides, he needed to get back to Arthur. The young boy would be wondering where he was. Rubbing his arms, he rushed out of the tent and back to daylight.

What a horrid old tent and what a strange old man. Alan shrugged and set off to buy a toffee apple and find his young companion.

It wasn't until he got home that he remembered the silver bell around his neck. *Stupid thing* thought Alan, and taking it off, he threw it into a tin at the back of a cupboard before going down to tea to tell his parents all about the stupid fair.

The episode was soon forgotten. Alan returned to school after the summer break, term times and holidays passing by in blocks of time to be endured. That time came quicker than even Alan could have hoped for.

He grew from a surly boy into a sour and hot-tempered young man. He barely made any friends at Eton and found people did not warm to him.

He spent his time at school idling away the time until he would go into business, but even that was delayed. In September 1939, Alan had just turned 18. He was about to study at Cambridge until the onset of war put everything on hold.

Alan signed up to be an officer with his grandfather's old regiment. Soon he was posted to the front in France.

His war was harsh but not as brutal as most, and he went through the war years unscathed. He was awarded many medals for bravery, not that he was honourable or brave. Somehow he always seemed to be the last man standing.

After the war, Alan went into his father's business and became very wealthy but turned even more cold and ruthless.
He bought himself a fine house on the outskirts of a prosperous town but never married.

As he grew older, the loneliness he'd shouldered as a young man pressed heavy, and bitterness took hold.

The years passed, and ill health caused him to retire…. a lonely, old man.

III

The first few months in Sheltered accommodation were difficult. He brooded on the past all winter, and the feeling of unease stayed with him. Yet, the dark days turned to spring, and his strength returned.

However, the door to the past remained open, and he drove to the village of his childhood, needing to rest his ghosts. He found it hadn't changed much, although the old shop had been converted to flats and the old quaintness had been replaced by 4 x4's and weekenders.

Once parked, he walked past the hedgerows and down a country lane where several people had gathered. Interested to see what was happening, he followed the throng, only to find it was the day of the annual fair. His steps slowed as he heard the carnival music in the distance, and for a moment, he was taken back to his childhood. His heart began to quicken as a strange fear prickled his conscience. Yet this was merely a coincidence – *what nonsense* – he thought. His body might be ailing, but his mind was still as sharp as ever.

The fair was much changed with the years. There were now mechanical rides that span and blurted out popular music, the sedate old steam horses long since retired. There were tents full of video games, prize bingo, a bouncy castle, and hot dog stalls.

The man wandered through the crowds, seeing the families smiling and having fun together. For the first time in his life, he felt a pain in his chest, the strange ache of regret.

Rounding a corner, he stopped in his tracks. At the far edge of the field stood a shabby canvas marquee. Sweat beaded his brow as he stepped forward. It couldn't be, surely not?

On an old tatty sign were scrawled the words 'Dr V Mysterious famous Freak Show Admittance 5 new pence. Alan wiped his brow with his handkerchief; surely it couldn't be the same show, the same man? Why that was almost seventy years ago.

A thin, reedy voice called out and made his blood chill.

"Alan, my dear chap, won't you step inside?"

He looked up, and stepping out of the tent, stood a wiry chap dressed in black.

"Alan, my friend, I have not seen you for many years. You have aged".

He gazed on incredulously. It couldn't be the same man. He must be long dead. It must be his son or grandson, but the resemblance was uncanny.

Before he could speak, he was escorted into the tent, a thin, wiry arm guiding his path.

The same familiar smell of decay and dampness filled his nostrils as if he'd stepped back in time and was a boy again.

The interior looked exactly the same. Shelves of bottles and jars lined up in rows, so many more than the last time he was here. Each one filled with the undefined, the macabre.

He was led along the rows without speaking.

"I expect you want to see your bottle," the man asked, grinning impishly. "It's a fine specimen."

Without waiting for an answer, the man reached up and pulled down a dusty old bottle, handing it to him.

The bottle looked so old. He wiped at the dust with his finger removing some of the dirt, allowing the brilliant purple to shine.

Through the glass, he could see something inside. He rubbed away more of the dirt to get a better look.

A large black distorted object with multiple tendrils was suspended in a thick, viscous liquid that clung to the sides of the bottle as he moved it around for a better view.

His hand now shook with fear.

"But what is it?" he asked, "What did you take from me all those years ago?

The old man merely smiled, his silver-grey eyes twinkling in the darkness.

"That, my friend," he whispered, "was your youth."

The End

Many years ago, Andy and I were invited to a formal dinner at Hatfield College Durham University. During dinner, I was seated next to the then Master of Hatfield College, and I promised to write him a story based on that evening. Here it is! The description of the dinner and college is very much as per my experience – with a story woven in for good measure.

Hatfield College

My return to Hatfield College was a grand occasion, having been invited to a formal senior common room dinner as one of the 'old boys.' I'd studied there for my degree 20 years previous. After finding some success in my chosen field, I had been lauded and decorated by many notable bodies. I dined out on my small celebrity status, and the whole affair had an air of amusing irony that I was most happy to take advantage of.

This was the first time I had met the new Master of the college. I say 'new,' but he had been serving in the post for13 years. In his 67th year, he was a surprisingly sprightly chap, with a fine head of hair sprinkled with grey, light blue eyes and a droopy, almost Mexican style moustache which gave him an air of eccentricity.
He also had a warm West Country accent that reminded me of open spaces and fresh, clean air. Far removed from the dry and dusty traditions and customs of academia.

Upon our first introduction Mr Brookes, the new Master, took my hand warmly and welcomed me back to my alma mater with heartfelt enthusiasm. I had left college 7 years before Mr Brookes became Master, but he greeted me as though welcoming back a beloved pupil to the fold.

His love and enthusiasm for the college were plain, and I have never yet met a man more dedicated to his work. He introduced me to the small gathering of professors and guests. His warmth radiated across the politics and ranks, bringing a glow to the craggy old Dons.

But his real love and fondest affections were saved for the students of Hatfield College, and in return, he had won their love and respect.

We lined up, ready for our grand entrance. As a special guest and fellow Hatfieldien, I was honoured to be seated next to the Master. A loud din from within the dining room announced it was time for our entrance. The students were already banging their cutlery in the old tradition to herald and speed the commencement of the meal. This 'spooning' was a ritual that had continued since the early 20th century and one I well remembered.

An immediate hush fell across the room as Mr Brookes entered, the rest of us following. The silence was part tradition and part respect, and we remained standing while a visiting German professor said grace

"Benedicte Deus, qui pascis nos a iuventute nostra et praebes cibum omni carni, reple gaudio et laetitia corda nostra, ut nos, quod satis est habentes, abundemus in omne opus bonum. Per Jesum Christum, Dominum Nostrum, cui tecum et Spiritu Sancto, sit omnis honos, laus et imperium in saecula saeculorum. Amen"

Not being a religious man, I lifted my head slightly during the blessing, looking over the bowed heads of the gathered Alumni. I beheld a sea of black cloaks, a murder of Ravens waiting to swoop down and devour the feast.

My eyes strayed briefly across the old Georgian building. The dining room was grandiose and had not changed much over the years. It was a little shabby, with a decorated overmantel, plaster ceiling, and painted wall panelling. Across one wall hung 15 portraits. The predecessors of Mr Brookes, spanning the last hundred and fifty years, viewed their beloved college with fixed eyes. The painting style, subject, and even frames gave away their era, the time when these painted faces were flesh and blood, breathing this ancient and hallowed air, just as I was.

A clamber of seats jolted me back to the matter at hand. The formalities were over, and the meal was about to start. Wine and soup were soon flowing, and looking to engage Mr Brookes, I brought up the subject of the portraits and asked when he would be honoured in such a manner.

The Master's eyes lit up. It was a popular and topical subject. He explained that the painting of his portrait was currently in discussion. An artist had been chosen, and he was to undertake the first sitting in a few weeks; the medium oils. He pointed to an empty place on the wall to his right, the place where his finished portrait would hang.

The rest of the evening passed in amiable spirits, the food delicious and the wine plenty. After coffee and brandy, we joined the students in the college bar for a rendition of the college song, accompanied by the beating of a large drum, rather untuneful but very rousing, and very soon, the old walls were vibrating with the sound of vivacious youth.

It was getting time for my train and departure, so I shook the hands of my fellow diners and said my fond farewells. The Master reminded me that he would call later the following week to discuss a joint research opportunity we had briefly touched on over dinner. Giving my thanks and best wishes, I left through the courtyard and under the arches beneath the chapel.

Passing through the hallowed gables, I glanced up and saw a plaque. It was half-lit by the lights in the quad. Instinctively I knew what it was, an eagle with wings spread and the inscription 'Sic transit Gloria Mundi; thus passes the glory of this world.

I thought of the young souls currently carousing in the bar. It seemed only a moment since I was they. My mind wandered morbidly to the portraits of the past Masters, once vibrant young men....

The cold air caused me to shudder, the drink was obviously making me maudlin, so I walked briskly through the crisp night air to the station, pulling the scarf tightly around my neck.

• • •

A couple of weeks later, I received a call from Mr Brookes. He would be free the following Wednesday afternoon. The meeting coincided with the first sitting of his portrait, but he would be free by 3 pm to meet in his rooms in college.

I arrived a little late on the said date, having missed my connection, and ran breathless to the college. Arriving at the Master's rooms, I could see him standing in one of the upper windows. He didn't seem to notice me and looked out into the distance. I approached the door but, finding it open, let myself in, shouting a hearty 'Hello' as I ventured inside. I waited in silence, not wanting to move further until acknowledged.

Finally, I heard a stirring above and the slow procession of footfall on the stairs until, at last, the Master appeared. He looked a little tired and somewhat distracted. I smiled, holding out my hand in greeting. The sight of me seemed to bring Brookes back from his reverie, and he shook his head, smiled, and laughed.

"My dear friend, forgive me; I am miles away," he said before explaining that he had just finished the first sitting for his portrait and had sat for almost 3 hours.

"Tiring business all this sitting around," he laughed, and we walked into his office to commence the business at hand.

Within 10 minutes and a strong cup of tea later, the Master was back to his usual self, and the incident was forgotten. I left him in the best of cheer, looking forward to our next meeting.

My next visit began on a cold wintry February morning. The sun cast a raw watery light across the gleaming snow. The dark outlines of trees were thrown rigidly against a seemingly innocent sky, branches blank and tight-lipped, vibrating on the merest hint of a breeze.

I trudged steadily up the hill towards the college, my steps deliberate and sure, picking my way through the drifts of snow.
Turning the corner towards the Master's house, I collided with a large dark-skinned man.
The man, in his middle age, I surmised, lost his footing and slipped solemnly onto the ground with a thud and a crunch into the snow.
The portfolio he'd been carrying flew out of his hands, the pages fanning through the air like a bird's wing before scattering across the frosty expanse.

A little shaken, I looked around, first at the scattered papers and then at the man. Quickly offering my arm, he was soon upright and quickly gathering his documents with a surprisingly lithe and nimble movement. Reaching down to help pick up the papers, I grasped the last sheet deftly in my gloved hand.

I was just about to pass the paper over when I glanced down at it and saw the beginnings of a sketch. As I focussed a little more, I could now make out a face. No, this was more than just any face. This was a sketch of the Master – Mr Brookes. It only took a few moments for me to realise that this must be the artist commissioned to execute the portrait. I handed the paper to the man who was now smiling at me, a wide grin bearing perfect teeth. I smiled back.

 "This is very good," I said, pointing to the picture and nodding. The man gave a small polite bow and answered in a low but clear tongue, "kukamata nafsi, I am capturing the soul, do you think"?

He held my gaze for a moment with magnificent hypnotic eyes. Then dropping his gaze, the man gave another polite bow and set off down the hill before I had time to answer.

I turned and watched him lightly pick his way through the snow, surprised at his agility, a Massai warrior setting off across a white desert.

The housekeeper let me into the Master's rooms, a steel-haired lady called Joan, who gave the overall impression of no-nonsense efficiency. She told me I would find the Master in his study. I took off my outer jacket, hung it in the hall, and made my way across the carpet, leaving behind a white trail of icy debris. Pausing before the study door, I listened. There was no noise, and I knocked lightly before entering.

The curtains were closed, and only a glimpse of the feeble light outside was visible. The room was cast in an afterthought of winter., as if the snow had fallen within the walls, casting an almost ghostly sheen over the contents. It took a while for my eyes to adjust, and finally spot the Master sitting at his desk.

He did not seem to notice me at first but sat, looking at something, or nothing, of that I could not tell. He was facing away from me, and not wanting to shock him, I coughed as if clearing my throat. I had to do this three times before the Master heard and acknowledged me. He turned slowly, his focus and mind evidently not in the room. His face looked thin, and his eyes absent. Within a moment, he withdrew from his self-absorption and glanced to where I was standing.

I don't think he recognised me at first, his eyes distant and glazed, but as focus gradually shifted, his pupils enlarged, taking in the face before him

"My dear fellow," he spoke in earnest, with the vigour of the sick to the healthy, and raised his left hand in acknowledgement to greet me. I took his hand, and it seemed small within my own, yet it clasped me with the strength and warmth of old friendship that spread to his eyes, taking me aback for a moment.

All I could do was gaze in shock at the Master, for he seemed to have aged in the short space since I'd last seen him. His hair was now mainly grey, and where he had once looked youthful and vibrant, his face wore a sagged, worn expression. I could barely keep my astonishment to myself.

"Good God, Man," I retorted, "Whatever has happened to you?"

He raised his eyes knowingly.

"My appearance, you mean?" he added, smiling, a sense of the 'old' Master returning.

"Yes, quite a queer thing, overnight I have grown into an old man, my youth catching up with me, I suppose?"

The Master smiled again, but without his former lightness, and his face grew serious.

"Helen thinks I should see a Doctor, but what should I tell him? That I'm growing old?"

I didn't know what to say, and sensing my unease, Brookes started to rise from his seat. I put out my hand to help him, which he dismissed frivolously with a wave of his hand.

"I think I can just about stand on my own, my young friend. Besides, I've been sitting for my portrait the last 2 hours, and I need to stretch my legs. Come walk around the room with me".

I stood aside while the Master rose to his feet, resisting the urge to put out my arm to help. This time, he took my arm. More out of friendship than need.

"Extraordinary chap, this painter fellow," he continued, now balanced and in his stride. "He's originally from Africa, you know, painting here on some kind of bursary."

The Master stood still in reflection for a second.

"Amazing eyes he has. It's almost as if he is looking right inside me, not just capturing the body, but something else, something…. deeper"?

He shook his head and laughed.

"I must be getting romantic in my dotage. Now to the task in hand, would you like some tea first? I'll ring for Joan".

I wanted to say something, to explain that I, too, had seen this man, if only briefly. I wanted to describe the peculiar effect that the artist had left on me, yet it seemed so silly, and thinking about the incident gave me a strange feeling that I wanted to forget.

I regret not discussing the matter further with the Master. It was to be the last time that I saw him.

Our next appointment was scheduled a fortnight later, but his wife Helen telephoned on the eve of the appointment, informing me that the Master had taken ill to his bed. It was likely to be a while before he would be fit enough to resume his normal duties.

He was dead within the month. Apparently, he had refused to see a doctor until it was too late. Even when called upon, the doctor failed to diagnose the illness. It was as if the Master had simply faded away.

. . .

I attended the funeral, a grand affair within the Cathedral, filled with the great and good of the academic world. Many old and new boys were in attendance, giving their last respects to a Master well-loved.

The college choir sang their sweetest, lifting the most agnostic amongst us to the heights of angels amongst the gothic pillars.

Tears pricked my eyes as eulogies were read from colleagues, friends, and pupils, and I, too, stood in silence with my own private recollections of a great man.

A few months later, a memorial dinner was held following a service of dedication in the senior common room at the College.

The dining room was just as it had been on my last visit, the decorated overmantel and plaster ceiling and painted wall panelling, and the portraits, of course.

I glanced along the row of paintings, and my eyes stopped at the wall to my right. Where once had been an empty space hung a picture covered with a red velvet curtain. The portrait of the Master was finished and would be unveiled at this ceremony.

I felt a sudden chill and recalled something unpleasant at the back of my mind, though I struggled to put form or shape to the thought. Before I could think more on the subject, there was a clanking of metal upon glass and a whispered hush around the seated diners.

The speeches began, a combination of warm, funny, and heartfelt. I could hardly hear the words above the pounding of my heart.

A fluttering of applause announced, at last, the unveiling of the portrait. We stood for the ceremony, and my mouth felt dry. I held onto the table for support with clammy hands, afraid my legs would give way to the rising sickness that was suddenly upon me.

As the deputy Master pulled a golden cord that swished back the red velvet curtains, I gazed at the portrait, open-mouthed.

There he was, the Master, benevolent and smiling down upon us, the light blue eyes surveying all from his vantage point. I stared at the face in astonishment. This wasn't just a painting. It was magnificent.

This was the Master.

It was almost as if the painter had captured his very soul!

The End

Based on camping trips to Mull. Andy loves kayaking in the sea surrounding Mull and Iona, and I have been out with him (just once). Great place for dolphin watching.

SAVED

The morning broke across a seamless sky. The golden spray of early sun lay across the granite boulders rising above the shoreline, casting their pink light towards the Sound of Iona.
The whole picture was stark, primaeval, a place to foster the spirits of the ancients, saints, and sinners alike.

Waves lapped with a gentle rhythm, slapping against the rocks with hypnotic resonance, while ewes and their young bleated towards the new sun. Wild birds called to greet the morning.

All was well beneath the heavens.

Tony looked at the canvas above. The early morning light shone through the skein of the tent, a blue light coating its contents. The tent roof arched its way above him, the noises of the outside world reaching his ears, yet all was still. In his mind, all was blank. He could hear the slow thud of his heart beating within him.

Without him.

It was a numbness of the senses. Tony had felt this way, this deadness, ever since Rachel had left him. That was over 3 months ago, and he was still suffering.

He could picture her. Just over a year ago, they had been together in this very same tent, on this exact spot. He had woken to see her beautiful face, unlined with sleep and huddled against the sleeping bag, warm and soft.

When she opened her eyes, his world had awoken too, his life complete with her. Without her, he was nothing…

Glancing at his watch, he sighed. It was only 04:30 am, but he couldn't sleep. Hadn't slept properly for 3 months. Without her softness beside him, her warm breath on the back of his neck, how could he?

It was time to make a move. Anyway, he needed a pee.

 Tony rose mechanically, peeling himself out of the sleeping bag, and shivered slightly.

Dressing quickly in yesterday's crumpled and slightly damp shorts and sweater, he unzipped the tent and stepped out into the world.

As bright as the light had been inside the tent, outside, the sun dazzled. Tony shielded his eyes against the reflection on the sea, a thousand mirrored wavelets dancing before him. The view was spectacular over the Sound of Iona, the Abbey standing alone and thoughtful in the distance.

Rachel would have loved this, thought Tony, but Rachel wasn't here.

Not a soul around, just the squares and rounds of canvas and tarpaulin, the residents sleeping soundly inside.

Walking to the sea, the freshness made him recoil from his gloom, and finding some rocks to shelter behind, relieved himself. It was too long a walk to the shower block, and besides, no one was around to see him.

Tony looked toward two identical tents by the edge of the rocks. Dave and Brian would be asleep for hours. He'd been persuaded by his friends to join them on a kayaking trip to help him forget, to move on with his life.

He thought of Rachel. It didn't seem to be working.

Yet today was beautiful. The water was still, glassy -a slight breeze rippling the surface. Ideal weather for a kayak trip.

The lads had talked of paddling out to Staffa the previous night, but they wouldn't be up for hours, especially after last night's drinking session.

Tony made up his mind. He would go out alone and paddle over to Iona and beyond.

Packing a few provisions and leaving a note for the boys saying he would be back in a few hours, Tony dragged his kayak from behind the tent down to the small beach and onto the water. He certainly looked the part after changing into his waterproofs, even if he hadn't been on the water for over 18 months.

He'd been too busy with Rachel.

Wading out into the sea, pushing the boat in front of him, he felt a strange sensation, a giddy feeling in the pit of his stomach. He'd forgotten how enjoyable this could be, alone in a boat with only the elements for company, and climbing into the boat, he paddled away from the shoreline and into the waves.

For a short while, all was well. Tony loved using his body; it had been so long since he'd been in a kayak, propelling himself along, man and boat as one. The cormorants wheeled overhead, gliding gracefully across the blue of early morning.

Yet as he rounded Iona, his thoughts drifted back to Rachel. She had loved this place.

Rachel. Her eyes shimmered on the water before him, and the beauty of the day began to slip away. He needed to be strong and fight against her memory, so he paddled quickly away, trying to put as much physical space as possible between him and the past.

He paddled fast, his body twisting as he pulled at the blade, detaching himself from her blue eyes, the soft timbre of her voice, the gentleness of her kiss.

His arms ached, but he kept on, determined that he would forget.

Tony stopped suddenly exhausted, drained of emotion and the sheer physical strain of propelling himself across the sea. He looked at his watch… 06:30, and he'd been on the water for over an hour. He looked around him. All was sea. Nothing but a grey, merciless heaving mass.

He had no idea how far he had come. The light breeze that had played easily on the shoreline now whipped at the surface, causing the boat to rock and dip with the rising and falling of the water. The sky had changed, a dark, brooding storm rolling in from the west.

Tony's thoughts no longer lingered on Rachel. Instead, fear gripped him from within. What a fool he'd been to come out alone, putting himself in danger and all because of a woman.

Anger began to mix with panic as the waves lapped with increasing vigour around the yellow kayak, a tiny insignificant speck on an eternity of grey.

Which way to paddle? Tony tried to remember the direction of the sun when he'd set off. Where was the sun now?

In desperation, he started to turn the boat around. Now choppy with the westerly wind, the sea tugged at his craft as he struggled against the current. He stopped again, his arms heavy with the effort, his stomach tight and knotted.

His brain hurt, trying to think of what to do. There was only one thing left.

As a last resort, he prayed to any god who might be listening and take pity on him. He was not a religious man, but he prayed to see another dawn. He prayed for life, his eyes closing with weariness. Was this how life would end? Alone and unloved…

After a few moments, he opened his eyes, an inner calm descending, a feeling of peace and resignation for whatever the fates decided.

The grey water was endless, like looking into eternity. Then, as he turned his head, something moved at the edge of his sightline. Tony turned, squinting into the distance. A dark shape leapt out of the water, then another and another.

A pod of dolphins.

Tony's heart thudded as he set off towards them, stopping at a distance and watching with delight, forgetting his predicament for a moment.

Sensing the boat, the creatures neared to investigate, lifting their smiling heads to view the strange craft. They grouped and swam behind the boat, looking back at Tony as if waiting.

They seemed to understand. They would guide him home.

Tony turned the boat around, the dolphins leading the way back to the shore.

Somehow deep inside, he knew he was safe. The healing had begun.

The End

This story is loosely based on when I first met Andy… I say loosely based! We did howl in the pub, though… Happy days!

Moonlight Becomes You

He glanced across the room. She was still there. Engaged in conversation, her face became agile, a thing of beauty. Her tiny heart-shaped face reminded him of an animal, a sphinx with high, prominent cheekbones chiselled from marble, a goddess from an ancient tribe. He'd noticed her a few times in the local pub but had never been close enough to speak. Besides, she always seemed so popular.

He had the feeling that she was different. There was something about her that stood out from the rest. Most of the time, she looked bored with the conversation and didn't seem to join the others in their idle chit-chat. He'd seen her a couple of times reading a book propped up on a barstool, fully engrossed in the pages.

He lifted his glass and drained the pint of its contents. Should he have another? After all, it was Friday night, a cold and damp October night at that. Why not?

Chris approached the bar, fishing into his pocket for just enough shrapnel to fund another round. The bar was heaving, and he stood with the others, eyes like hawks following the barmaid in the hope of being served.

As he stood waiting, he looked around. She'd gone. The crowd of girls were still there, but she had gone. He felt his heart sink and a disappointment rise within. How ridiculous. He didn't even know this girl but somehow felt her loss. Perhaps he'd been too lonely of late.

Eventually, the barmaid turned her fixed smile and served him another pint of his favourite, crisp pale ale. His only pleasure these days. He glanced at the row of sad old men lining the bar and sighed.

God, was this his life now, work and beer?

Head down, he turned from the bar, concentrating on not spilling the beer but stopped in his tracks as a queer sensation passed through his body like a warming sun.

The beer must be good!

He noticed a soft scent in the air above the beer and body odour. Not the usual harsh smell of cheap perfume, but something subtle, natural. He stopped, aware of someone in front of him, and lifted his eyes from the glass.

The girl was standing in his path, and Chris felt his head sway as an awkwardness spread over him. His hand jerked, swilling a glug of beer over the rim of his glass and onto his shoes. He looked up, wishing for one moment that he wasn't there. The girl was smiling at him.

"Hi," she smiled, "sorry, I didn't mean to startle you."

It was the first time Chris had seen the girl up close. She had blue-green eyes and a small nose that twitched, occasionally emphasising her feline features. Her hair was dark and curled around small ears.

He liked this face. He liked it a lot.

"Try not to get your feet too wet," the eyes flashed back with humour.

Chris couldn't help but smile. He looked down at his faded and scuffed shoes, now covered in dark spots, contrasting widely with the girl's smart black heeled boots, gleaming, pristine.

He needed something to say, and the beer hadn't quite loosened his tongue.

"Can I get you a drink?" he looked at her, hopefully. At least it was a start.

She looked back into his eyes, still smiling. "Great, I'll have a large glass of red, please."

Standing at the bar, he pulled himself together. What was wrong with him? He wasn't usually this tongue-tied.

"That will be £3.60," shouted the barmaid above the rising noise.

Chris had a sinking feeling. He'd just managed to pull together enough change for his last pint and hadn't intended to be out this long. His left hand rummaged in his back pocket, his heart sinking deeper and deeper as he felt the outline of two coins.

He pulled out his hand. 15p, one 10p and one 5p.

"£3.60," shouted the barmaid again. Chris looked at her; he looked through her, feeling the sweat spread across his brow, mouth dry, despite the two pints of beer. He studied the barmaid. She looked old, worn, her peroxide hair fading into the yellowing wallpaper, the smoker's legacy. The face was pale, transparent, with a covering of powder that sat in every crease and line of her tired skin, like a road map of her life.

Chris froze. What to do? The barmaid in front of him, the girl behind. He wanted to disappear. Was this a dream, a nightmare of the first order?

He heard a snorting noise behind, and then a slim hand appeared holding out a £10 note, crisp and clean.

"Take it from this…and another pint, please," the voice whispered, tinkling as soft and low as the murmuring river he heard through his window at night.

He could tell by the rhythm in her voice that she was smiling.

She moved beside him, slipping her tiny frame comfortably between the bar and his left arm. He felt the warmth radiate from her like an animal, her scent drifting around him, this time more intense, primitive yet subtle. He felt it permeate his thoughts, lifting him into an enchanted place.

"Your pint?" quizzed the soft voice behind his left ear.

Chris stood his mind elsewhere.

What was the matter with him? He seemed almost bewitched by this girl.

Picking up his pint, he turned to face her. She was so close that he felt the gentlest stroke of breath against his neck. She stood slightly smaller than him, her eyes watching him with catlike intensity.

She must have sensed his awkwardness, for she withdrew slightly, returning to her own space.

Chris took a gulp of his pint and glanced back at the girl through the glass, raising the beer to his mouth. She was smiling. No, she wasn't smiling; she was laughing. Not a dainty girly giggle but a whole-hearted guffaw. Her eyes crinkled, and her hands flew up to her face to try and hide her merriment.

"I'm so sorry," she struggled to say between the laughter, lifting her eyes up to his like a naughty schoolgirl. Her face was so beautiful that he felt like reaching out and kissing her, but instead, he merely smiled back.

"Sorry about the drink. I didn't intend on staying out long. I owe you one".

The girl smiled back. She didn't want him to keep thinking of his embarrassment. She changed the subject.

"It's a beautiful full moon tonight. I saw it hanging in the trees high up over the hill."

On his short walk to the pub, Chris had noticed the bright orb hanging low in the sky. He'd always been fascinated by the moon, and its mysteries and magic had enthralled him over the years.

He nodded in acknowledgement.

 "Yes, I saw it. I'll be howling later," he smirked back while thinking what a stupid thing to say. The girl's eyes lit up.

"Really, me too," she replied and, smiling back, opened her perfect mouth, showing the merest hint of white teeth, and let out a small howl.

Chris was taken aback at first. She was a funny thing. Not the merest hint of embarrassment or awkwardness about her. Open with a sense of innocence, well, almost.

"I'll be walking up on the hill with the dog later. Maybe you'd like to come?" Chris looked into his glass, taken aback by his sudden boldness.

The girl shrugged. "Not tonight, but maybe some other time?"

There followed a period of silence where Chris wished he'd never asked the question -stupid, stupid with a capital S.

"Well, I'll have to be going. Thanks for the drink", the girl added with a cheeky grin, and the irony was not wasted on him.

With that, she was gone.

Chris turned around and watched her leave, taking all her life and light out into the dark night.

His stomach lurched as he looked around. As if awakening from a troubled sleep, he was suddenly hit by the shabby and sullied atmosphere of the place. The loud and leery drunks, the ugliness of it all. He felt the loneliness spreading until his entire body was aching. Putting the half-finished pint onto the bar, he pushed through the drunken crowd.

He had to find the girl.

Rushing from the light into the darkness made him giddy, and he leant against an outside wall to get his breath, his heart racing wildly.

What was he doing?

He scanned the empty street, peering through the lights and the darkness beyond. There was no sign of the girl. There were two paths to take, but which had she followed?

A low whine alerted him to his dog, still tied to the railing, waiting patiently for its master.

The dog nuzzled his hands. The warmth of the fur and the wagging tail of unquestioning love almost brought him to tears. Untying the dog, they set off together.

Instinctively, he turned to the right, the path less trod. Let the moon be his guide.

Hurrying along the quiet street, his footsteps vibrated off the hard pavement and echoed through the still night air, the dog tripping beside him like a shadow. He stopped and looked around, his breath smoky in the cold air. She was nowhere to be seen. He had taken the wrong path after all and didn't even know where she lived.

Looking up at the sky in desperation, he sent out a heartfelt plea to whatever magic existed in the heavens. And then he spotted her. Or spotted something, a lone figure walking on the hillside, lit by the pale lunar glow.

Although the figure was some way away, he knew it was her. She pulled him towards her with an invisible cord.

Turning off the road, they made their way towards the path that led up the hill.

What was the matter with him? Had he become some kind of stalker?

But he couldn't stop now. The lure of the girl was too strong.

Man and dog walked silently up the slope towards the moon, which hung so low they could almost touch it.

At the top, Chris looked around. The beauty of the night was not lost on him. The trees and foliage swathed in enchantment.

But where was the girl? He had definitely seen her come this way. The top of the hill was flat and deserted.

Suddenly the dog began to whine and snarl, jumping into the air. Something was howling, a low soft sound piercing the darkness, increasing in volume and pitch. He turned quickly, and there standing quietly behind him was the girl.

She looked more beautiful than before. Her green eyes glinting and sparkling like emeralds, the moonlight throwing shadows across her angular features.

Her brow slightly furrowed as she looked at him and her lips parted, ready to speak.

Yet before her words could spill into the air, the dog pulled free and was upon her. Snapping and snarling, it leapt at her throat, knocking her to the ground. Chris stared in amazement. He tried to kick the dog away from the girl, but its hold was too strong, too fierce.

It was several minutes before he managed to haul the dog away, and it slunk off into the bushes, tail between its legs.

The girl lay still on the ground, pale and lifeless in the moonlight. The dog had ripped at her throat, and she was dead. Chris looked on in disbelief. This could not be happening to him. He knelt down and touched her beautiful face. She was still warm with the last traces of life.

Taking off his coat, he gently laid it over the body before sitting next to her on the damp grass and began to howl into the void.

The night drew on. Soon it would be morning. He had to leave. Slowly picking himself off the ground, he whistled for the dog before setting off slowly down the slope and headed for home, leaving behind the body of the beautiful wolf.

It was a lonely life, living on his own, but perhaps this was best. The dog had sensed it from the start – had known better than him. This was a small village with no room for rivals.

There was, after all, room for only one werewolf in this village…

The End

This story is based on a doll we had at home while growing up. I was terrified of it and still am…I wonder where it is now!

Click Clack

Thrice the brinded cat hath mew'd
Thrice and once, the hedge- pig whined
Harpier cries 'Tis time, 'tis time.

I don't know what made me remember. Unearthing 70 years of memories isn't easy, but sometimes, by chance, something in the present illuminates the past.

I'd been drifting in and out of sleep for most of the day. In the hospital, there was little to do except sleep. Magazines had ceased to amuse me. A couple of books remained half-read due to the deterioration of my eyesight, despite the larger print.

One day the endings would be forever lost to me.

Sleeping most of the day and wide awake at night had been the pattern of the last week. The nights were the worst. Endless and un-blinkered, gazing at the harsh strips of emergency lighting, listening to the hacking coughs and murmurs of fellow patients.

Death, where is thy sting!

I had very few visitors. Friends were either dead or no longer in touch. Perhaps the odd card at Christmas, if I was lucky. I had a daughter living on the opposite side of the world who wouldn't take kindly to rushing back home to see her old Mum in hospital, not unless it was for something gainful like the reading of a will.

Friends… maybe that had started me thinking? Joyce and Beryl had been my best friends throughout school and even into our early married lives. Though jobs and families had moved us around the country, we stayed close. Was it only five years ago that we had met to celebrate our joint 65th birthdays? Five years. Five short years, and now they were both dead.

Our merry trio had been named 'the three witches' by our fellow pupils at school. Shakespeare had been heavy on the curriculum, and Macbeth had featured in the first term, the nickname holding fast.

We were wild children. All at a private girl's school during the war, our parents flung across the globe, either as part of the war effort or spreading the word of god.

In the early days, we three had formed a tight band of sisters. We deserved the label ' the three witches' with our long flowing hair and propensity for mischief.

And now there was one. One little witch. I don't think I'd realised how much I missed my friends until now.

Joyce had been in good health. That's why it had been such a shock. Her death was an accident, they said. Somehow she had just stepped into the road, and it was over, just like that. Dead. Not even a busy road.

It had been a woman driver, not her fault, the papers said. There were no witnesses, but plenty of people had rushed from their shopping to help. After the impact, Joyce had lived for a short while but was dead from severe chest injuries by the time the ambulance came.

The lady driver had stayed with Joyce during her last moments. At least she hadn't died alone.

Maybe I would die alone in the hospital? *What a ridiculous notion.* I suppose I was just feeling sorry for myself.

For Beryl, it had been different. The fire service concluded that the incident was caused by a faulty electrical appliance. She had been in good health too, or so she had told us at our last reunion. Said she had never felt better. It was only a few weeks after our 65th birthday celebrations. I shudder to think of her death. She was still conscious when they found her, but her body had been badly burnt. Like Joyce, a female firefighter had been there at her last moments. I hoped it had given Beryl some small comfort.

I remember the three of us laughing loudly, so clearly in my mind, only a few years ago. We had looked even more like three witches at our celebration with wrinkles and greying hair. Double, double toil and trouble; Fire burn and cauldron bubble. We had cackled, reciting Shakespeare's words to ward off Hitler's bombs and the horrors of war we tried to forget.

It was Joyce who had first remembered. Although I think we had all remembered but had chosen not to.

It was 31st October 1944, Halloween, and we were 12 years old. Our small girlish coven wanted to celebrate the date with something special. Beryl, the most intense of the three, wanted to perform a sacrifice. She had become obsessed after reading a book on the subject, secreted from her father's substantial library from his travels abroad.

Joyce and I had a more sensible and less bloodthirsty approach. Instead of a sacrifice, why didn't we resurrect something? Bring life, not death… but to what? We didn't have an odd corpse lying around, and we weren't allowed to keep pets at school, so there was no pet cemetery to raid. It all looked hopeless then Beryl had an idea.

Miranda! Why didn't we bring Miranda to life?

I had been given a very large plastic doll for my 10th birthday and had named her Miranda. She had poseable arms and legs, a painted mouth, lips slightly ajar showing a tooth, and huge glass blue eyes with thick black eyelashes. Her eyes closed and opened if you rocked her to and fro, making a click-clack sound.

I had never liked Miranda. Her hard, brittle plastic body made her impossible to nurse like a baby, and I could almost feel her sleepless glassy gaze on me as night fell across the dormitory.

I wasn't happy with the plan but consented, not wanting to spoil the fun or appear to be a baby.

'Diabolus, diabolus addo ut vita. Resurrectio,' Beryl had remembered the spell and recited it with a flourish at our reunion.

She had been very keen on Latin at school and composed the spell. 'Satan, Satan, bring life, Resurrect.'

The day of the 31st comes back clearly. We had wanted a fire in the woods at night but instead would have to sneak out mid-afternoon due to our early curfew and blackout regime.

It was a Tuesday and lessons finished at 3 pm. We looked the part, wearing cloaks made from spare blackout material and carrying long bamboo canes stolen from the garden shed. The old school was set in large grounds, and we quickly found a small copse far away from the school and the prying eyes of the mistresses.

It had been a dry autumn, and we quickly gathered enough broken branches and dry leaves to make a small fire. The sky was steely grey, and the air cold. I can still feel the excitement of our secret plan.

We soon had the fire lit and joined hands as we slowly skipped around the flames chanting, "Double double toil and trouble; Fire burn and cauldron bubble."

Louder and faster, we spun around in our circle, gripping each other's hands tightly, working ourselves into an adolescent frenzy. Our school was strict and straight-laced, and our pent-up energy burst free.
Falling to the ground, we giggled helplessly in the way only young girls can, our hair wild, cheeks glowing, and hearts beating fast beneath the black cloaks.

Joyce was the first to stand. Having played leading parts in the school play, she excelled in her witchy role. In a solemn voice, she spoke, "And now the time has cometh; bring forth the subject for Resurrection. Naked came I out of my mother's womb, and naked shall I return thither: the LORD shall give, and the LORD shall take away; blessed be the name of the LORD".

Joyce's father was a minister serving overseas, and she loved the ritual and performance of Christianity, albeit ours was quite an unholy affair.

Unwrapping Miranda from her blanket, the pink plastic body glowed almost transparent in the firelight. We made a makeshift altar above the fire using a metal tripod as the base to keep her away from the flames. The doll was placed in a cardboard box on top of the tripod, her arms and legs in the air, her eyes closed

"We need blood," shouted the gruesome Beryl, thinking of the images in her father's books. Joyce and I looked at each other warily.

"Just a drop to splash on her body to help the spell," Beryl gushed enthusiastically.

Joyce and I were not keen on the idea, especially when Beryl drew a penknife from her pocket. We both gasped.

"Babies" was Beryl's retort, and she quickly opened the blade and pulled it across one of her fingers.

Immediately a line of blood sprang from the light wound, crimson against her pale skin. She held her finger above the makeshift altar, and a drop of blood splashed across the pale chest of Miranda, running down her side like a Christ wound. Our eyes widened. Real blood, this was exciting.

Then the spell began in earnest. Beryl started the recitation, having taken the credit for composing the words. "Diabolus, diabolus addo ut vita. Resurrectio," she spoke loudly and solemnly.

"Diabolus, diabolus addo ut vita.Resurrectio". Joyce and I joined in the chanting, and, holding each other's hands, we solemnly walked around the fire.

"Diabolus, diabolus addo ut vita.Resurrectio, Diabolus, diabolus addo ut vita. Resurrectio."

We must have looked a queer spectacle, three girls in black cloaks dancing around a fire. It was getting chilly, and the sky was beginning to darken. After about 5 minutes, we felt cold, and much of our initial enthusiasm started to wane.

It was then that a funny thing happened.

Looking back, I think it must have been something to do with the heat from the fire, for Miranda's eyes opened suddenly.

Click.

There she lay, her glassy blue eyes staring into the dying light of the day. We all stopped in silence. Our hearts were beating fast. Before anyone could speak, a gust of wind lifted the blaze of the fire high up the legs of the tripod, and the cardboard box holding Miranda caught light.

The flames quickly took hold, engulfing the doll, and the panic started.

Beryl picked up her cane and tried to knock the box away from the fire. Instead, the box collapsed into the fire along with the doll.

At that point, a horrible screeching noise emitted from the doll. It must have been the air squeezing out of the hollow plastic body, but it meant only one thing to us.

We had brought Miranda to life, and now she was burning to death.

Joyce started screaming, convinced we had summoned the devil, picked up her stick, and started beating the melting corpse across the chest, making deep gashes across the now sticky mass.

I didn't know what to do. The hissing sound was still emitting from the body as Miranda's face began to melt. The toothy open mouth dripped into the head cavity, the eyes remained open, unblinking, a melting, ghoulish mask.

I could no longer look at the face and plunged my stick into the gooey mass, gouging easily through the face and pushing the eyes out of the sockets, the plastic skin coating the end of my cane. It could only have lasted a few moments. The cheap plastic melted quickly. All that was left were the two glass eyes, now opaque and blind. I kicked them away into the long grass.

It was over. We looked at each other and giggled. Not out of fun but hysteria. Nothing was said about the episode, and the amateur coven was forgotten.

It would be 51 years later before the incident was mentioned again at our 65th joint birthday celebrations, with Joyce reciting, "Diabolus, diabolus addo ut vita. Resurrectio".

How silly it now seemed. We raised our glasses of champagne to friendship and lost youth.

"Diabolus, diabolus addo ut vita. Resurrectio" may we all be given life.

And that was only a few years ago. And now Joyce and Beryl were dead, and I was in the hospital. Not that my hospitalisation was considered life-threatening. I had an advanced deteriorating eye condition, and surgery was my last chance to save the little sight I had.

All through that night, my mind dwelt on the past, not wanting to think of the next day, the operation, and the possible consequences.

Eventually, daylight began to creep into the ward, heralding the day. The breakfast trolleys were wheeled around the ward, but no food or drink for me. Peering out of my bed, I could make out the hazy shapes of patients and blots of colour that I presumed were flowers.

The doctor and surgeon came and chatted to me early morning about the op. Although they were upbeat, it was made clear that there was a fifty percent chance the operation could leave me blind.

They came to fetch me just after ten.

I was gowned and on the trolley and down to the theatre in no time. While waiting, I was given an injection, something to relax me. A 'gin and tonic' the doctor had joked.

The injection began to take effect, and I felt a warm, sinking sensation. I heard the door open. It must be time.

Two people in scrubs approached. I couldn't see clearly and was almost asleep. I heard a male voice speaking as if in a dream...

"Mrs Taylor ...Mrs Taylor, here is Nurse Smith, Miranda. She will take care of you."

Two large blue eyes looked down at me from above a green facial mask.

The last image I would ever see.

Click Clack.

The End

I wrote this for a friend and colleague for a bit of fun – who is also a wedding singer (and part-time fabulous 70's & 80's Glam Rock star too!)

The Wedding Singer

Kezia was Rachel's best friend, or that's how it seemed to the world. They'd been friends since primary school and inseparable ever since. Twenty years to be exact. For two decades, they'd been bosom buddies.

They shared the same taste in clothes, music, make-up, and men.

That was unfortunate for poor Kezia, for while she was small, fat, and mousey, Rachel had grown into a leggy, blonde stunner.

Despite this fact, Kezia and Rachel remained firm friends.

There had been only one tiny blip in their relationship. This occurred when Rachel became engaged to the fabulous Mark.

Mark was 6ft 2", with dark curly hair and magnificent eyes that could leave a girl breathless at 50 paces.

Regrettably, Kezia had secretly been in love with Mark long before he and Rachel met. It had been a mad, restless hope of a love that kept Kezia awake at night and dreaming by day.

Unwittingly, Kezia had introduced the two while she and Rachel were out shopping in town one Saturday afternoon. Mark was a private patient at the clinic where Kezia was a nurse and a bit of a health freak in an OCD kind of way. He had frequent 'general health' checkups at the clinic, and Kezia had got to know him quite well.

She'd managed to keep this fine specimen to herself for a couple of years, away from the beautiful Rachel.

The relationship was purely platonic, of course. Kezia knew she had no chance but still had her dreams.

But there he was, one Saturday afternoon as they were shopping, strolling around the chilled food section of Marks & Spencers, looking all gorgeous and single
.

It had been love at first sight for Rachel and Mark.

And naturally, a year later, they were to be married.

Kezia was asked to be Matron of Honour, and *matron* was a great word to pigeonhole the frumpy Kezia.

She'd been without a boyfriend for the last five years. Truth be told, she hadn't really had a boyfriend, only a drunken Christmas snog with the sweaty guy from IT two years ago and, of course, Adrian Godfrey. Still, she'd only been six years old and guessed that didn't really count.

Anyway, he'd flicked bogies at her.

The bridesmaid dress was peach, satin, tight-fitting, and highly unflattering.

Kezia could hardly wait.

As part of the service, Rachel asked Kezia to sing, to fill the pause between the vows and the signing of the register. Despite her looks, Kezia had the voice of an angel.

Reluctantly she agreed, but then, Rachel was her best friend.

Probably her only friend.

Kezia even helped Rachel choose the song - *Ave Maria* - arranged to show off her full vocal range.

She started taking lessons, especially for the event, to deliver the ultimate performance for her dearest friend...even though she was marrying the man of *HER* dreams.

She was already improving her vocal range to stretch comfortably over four octaves. Her music teacher said that with hard work and dedication, she might even hit the five-octave range like her heroine, Yma Sumak, who in the 1950s was well known for her ability to shatter glass with her high notes.

It was six months before the wedding, and Kezia practised her singing daily, her confidence and ability growing.

Eventually, the big day arrived. A perfect day, all blue skies and sunshine.

Mark and Rachel really were *the beautiful people.*

The perfect couple, everyone whispered as the bride glided down the aisle. At the same time, Kezia stood at the back, in the shadows, sweat staining the peach satin that was uncomfortably bunched beneath her arms. She'd put on a few pounds since the fitting, and the Bride's Mother had lent a hand to squeeze her fleshy mass inside the delicate fabric, catching the ripples of skin as she tugged the zip finally closed.

Feeling stifled in the heat, Kezia stretched and, as she did, felt the seams around her bosom snap and pull open.

Never mind, she was past caring how she looked, plus it felt a lot more comfortable this way. She could hide behind her flowers, and it would give her room to breathe during her solo.

Walking behind the golden couple, she heard the gasps of admiration, obviously not aimed at her.

Yet, Kezia's moment was to come. After the vows, the exchange of rings, and the all-important kiss, it would be her turn to shine, her moment, briefly in the spotlight.

Her heart began to pound. Could she do it? Could she go through with it?

All those hours of practice.

Standing at the front of the church, suddenly, all eyes were upon her.

There was no music, just the voice. Kezia took a deep breath, feeling the rise of her chest….

The purity of the solo rose to the roof, confirming to those within, even if for a short time, that God must exist.

It was a moment of sheer pleasure, absolution resounding in every note.

The voice rose higher and higher, the pitch ascending to the heavens, ringing the ears and vibrating the pews. Even the saints looking down from the windows, resplendent in a golden holy light, seemed in awe of this strange figure with the voice of an angel.

The moment was coming. Kezia felt her diaphragm lift and expand, her voice mounting until there was nothing but the note.

And there it was, the elusive high C, the highest C, reverberating clear and shrill among the glass of the ceiling lights as it dazzled and sparkled through the air.

The note was held… the resonance building until all was one with the pure vibration of sound.

Then it happened.

The groom, the lovely groom Mark, collapsed. An aneurism, they said. He didn't have a chance. It could have happened at any time, a weak artery wall. Probably the stress of the wedding. No one could have known,

Except for Kezia, that is.

Mark's medical records had been enlightening. If a high-pitched note could shatter glass, what would it do to the frail human form?

Well, they do say all is fair in love and war, especially between friends!

The End

There are two themes interwoven here – one on the theme of Remembrance Day and the other – thinking about the loss of memory – particularly around Alzheimer's. My dad's elder brother was in the RAF and shot down- presumed dead in WW2 and never got to see his child. My mum died of Alzheimer's in 2020.

Remembrance

Mary fastened up her coat carefully. Large buttons, suitable for stiff fingers. It was a good coat, well made with lots of wool. It wasn't new. In fact, it was second-hand. It had been her mother's best winter coat when she was alive.

It had been hanging in the wardrobe just after the funeral and seemed a shame to waste such a good coat.
That seemed a long time ago now. It must be fifteen years at least.

Funny how you can remember things that happened all that time ago yet can't even remember what you just had for breakfast.

Mary remembered the good old days, not just fifteen years ago, but back some 80 odd years. Her childhood during the war...

. . .

Ted buttoned up his RAF uniform, the grey-blue material matching the steeliness of his eyes. Another day of the war, another flight, but at least he would be home in a few more weeks. Jeannie was about to give birth, and it would be their first. He had only been married a year. Bloody war. Hopefully, it would be over soon, and then he could get on with the rest of his life.

Ted pulled the flight jacket around him. The air was cold. Feeling in his pocket, he pulled out the tatty photograph and kissed it for luck before setting out into the frosty night...

. . .

It was funny remembering all those years ago, crystal clear memories. Running over the fields to the pictures on a Saturday morning, saving the penny bus fare to buy an apple, fishing for tiddlers in the local canal, happy days, or so they seemed.

Now, where was her bag? Mary looked around. Where had she put it? She was constantly losing things these days, putting things down, putting things away, then forgetting where she'd put them.

Of course, her mother had started that way. She'd hardly been able to speak in the end. Vascular Dementia, they'd said. It all seemed such a long time ago now. In the end, she hadn't even recognised Mary.

Her mother, Jeanie, had been in the kitchen when it happened. She could remember being told as a young girl, even when she'd forgotten everything else.

A telegram '*We regret to inform you... missing in action, presumed dead*', just a few bleak words to break her mother's heart, to leave the child without a father.

Even when her mother had forgotten the names and the faces, the sadness and the loss remained...

• • •

Ted knew the end had come, shot down mid-flight. He fought at the controls, burning and raging in those few brief moments before the darkness came. Weeping for his short life, the lost future, Jeanie... the child he would never see...

• • •

Mary studied her face in the mirror, the blue-grey eyes, the powdered cheeks, and a hint of lipstick. She was getting more like her mother every day. Except for the eyes, she had her father's eyes, or so they said. He'd been killed in the war before she was born.

Now, where was she going? She had put her coat on, so she must be going somewhere.

Looking down, Mary smiled. Now she remembered. Picking up the pin, she fixed the red and black poppy into the lapel of her coat.

Lest we Forget

The End

Like most stories, this one has an element of truth. In fact, more than an element. This did happen to me at Belsay Hall in Northumberland – although wrapped around the framework of a story.

Eostre (Goddess of the Spring)

Suddenly it all fell into place, the circle complete.

The sudden realisation made her giddy, and she laughed out loud at finally finding a release for her past sorrow.

And now she was back where it had begun… yet she was not thinking of the present. Instead, her mind travelled back - nine years into the past, or in the words of L.P. Hartley, a foreign country.

. . .

The day had been bright. The sun pulled her out of doors to feel the warmth upon her winter skin.

That was the reason for the excursion to Belsay Hall. Having heard so much about the gardens, especially the Rhododendrons, she finally decided to go and see them.

Apart from the splendour of the flora, she knew very little of the place, and it seemed the ideal way to spend a fine afternoon in early June.

Besides, a gloom had started to spread over her, and she needed restoration.

The journey was a little over half an hour and took four of them through the winding roads of the Northumberland countryside.

The fields stretched out in late spring glory, chartreuse, and emerald, where the shafts of sunlight caught the land, teal, and olive in the dips and hollows.

The reds and violets of campion and foxgloves seemed artificially rouged across the honest green scape that rolled before them, an unending tumble of patched farmland and edgeless moor.

They were soon upon signs for Belsay Hall, and two or three sweeping turns found them on the approach. The sun blazed across their vision-obscuring everything in its headlamp. She squinted into the glare, making out the forms of trees and bushes lining the gravelled entrance, dark shadows against the intense brightness.

Belsay was built in the early 19th century in the Greek style. A solid-looking building bearing two large pillars at the entrance and made of stone from the quarry contained within its grounds.

The golden walls shimmered behind the day's heat, reflecting the light and creating a luminous and ethereal temple to the gods.

As splendid as the house appeared, the glory of the day beckoned them outdoors, and the purpose of the visit was to view the Rhododendrons.

They parked the car quickly– the place was deserted. The beauty of the day lost on office workers who could only dream of the outdoors.

Crunching along the pathway, they walked around the side of the main building, the hall standing tranquil in splendid isolation with a tomb-like austerity.

The morning was reaching its peak, the sun swirling across the cornflower sky. The woman stood for a moment feeling the glow and warmth on her face, lost in the moment.

Closing her eyes, she breathed deeply. Her husband and friends had already walked ahead, and she stood alone without the limits of time, her mind free and floating in the soft, mellow air.

The distant calling of her name brought her back, and opening her eyes, she looked around. The others were already out of sight, lost behind the looming edifice of the hall.

She walked slowly in the direction of the voices, lost in her reverie – lifting her arms in praise to the sun god, luxuriating in the first real warmth of the year. As she rounded the corner, she stopped dead – unprepared for the sight.
Below her, the giant rose trees splayed, swathing the stage beyond in a sensory phenomenon - a red-blue spectrum dashed across the garden canvas with genius strokes.

The experience made her light-headed - the flora - intoxicating and beckoning, pulling her down under the heat. She could almost sense the cool protection of the flower heads, the heavy sweet smell lulling her into the darkness of sleep and beyond.

The woman swayed with nature; she was nature and felt the fertile twist of Isis beneath the earth bringing new life with the sun. Yet, she was still awaiting her Spring, and the waiting made her sad.

Suddenly tired, she sat down, overlooking the Rhododendrons spreading her long legs over the soft grass and closing her eyes. The sun licked at her winter wounds, and as the birds called softly amongst the trees, the woman began to doze, feeling life pulsing in the earth below.

A hand brushing gently across her face brought her back, and blinking away the sunshine, she smiled up at the familiar faces. They were off to have tea. Would she join them?

Soon ... soon, her hand waved them away, hoping for a few more moments alone.

She dozed a while longer but, on waking - sat up and looked at her watch. The sun had swung around the heavens, and another half hour had passed. Incredibly, the heat was still rising. Once again, she felt a lightness, a giddiness at being in the sun too long. Apart from the flora below, the landscape shimmered in the early summer, the heat rising and contorting the air.

Behind her, the hall stood patiently, waiting, cool in its shadow, and rising, she walked back to the main entrance.

 From this angle, the hall looked more like a museum than a dwelling, the imposing stone steps leading beyond the Grecian pillars and into the building.

She hesitated on the steps. The place was open to the public, yet it looked empty. The others must still be having tea. She would join them soon, but first, she wanted to experience the cool shade of the old house by herself.

Walking up the steps and out of the sun, her flesh became goose pricked, her footsteps echoing on the solid wooden floor.

The main entrance was arranged and supported on all sides with a host of chiselled columns from floor to ceiling, each one topped with a scroll to emphasise the Grecian grandeur. The house itself was unfurnished. The life and vibrancy long absorbed into the walls and stonework.

She climbed the stone staircase with its spider's web ironwork and along the mezzanine landing to a large wooden door that was slightly open, causing a v of light to cunningly streak across the shaded recess.

Pushing the heavy door open, she paused, taking in her first impressions.

The room was light and airy, with four double sash windows running from floor to ceiling. Walking over to take in the view, she was struck once again by the solitude of the house.

 Dust particles hung, suspended in the golden voile of sunlight streaming in layers across the floor.

The room looked out onto the south side of the gardens with a view of the Rhododendrons and Quarry Gardens.
This must have been the master bedroom of the house. What a pleasure to have woken to that view in any season.

But now, the room was empty as the rest of the house. The walls were bare save for a scratching of wallpaper, a faded flowery relic of another era.

The woman touched the walls. They were cold and lifeless. What had happened to the spirit of the house?

Stepping through an adjoining door into a smaller room, she embraced the same splendid view, but once again, it was empty. She looked at a small plaque on the wall. The room had been the old nursery.

Walking back down the stairs, melancholic and morose thoughts started to gather. She felt the loss and emptiness of the house as if it were her own, a poor, barren creature lying dormant awaiting the gift of life.

Wandering into one of the main rooms, the Ballroom, she supposed from its generous space, she stood alone in the centre, feeling at odds with herself as the gloomy thoughts collected.

Lowering her head, she closed her eyes for a few seconds. Maybe she'd been out in the sun too long? All was quiet, yet she noticed a slight shift in the air as if someone had opened the door.

She opened her eyes as a cool breeze entered the room, and a small child ran past and disappeared behind her

Surprised, she turned to catch sight of the infant, but it was too late; the child had gone, probably through the door behind her. She didn't know whether it was a boy or girl and closed her eyes to try and remember.

It had all happened so quickly...

Upon hearing footsteps, she opened my eyes. Her party had returned to find her. She laughed, relieved to be with company again, and started to tell them of the child and how it had startled her.

They looked back with blank faces. There was no child. They were the only party left in the house and grounds. With a sudden realisation, she knew there had been no noise, no light footsteps echoing across the floor.

 It had been the vague impression, not a solid form, more of a blur like something seen when travelling fast from a car window or a train.

Closing her eyes, she saw once again the blur, the whirl of energy as it rushed beyond her.

• • •

That was nine years ago. Standing in the very same room at Belsay Hall had brought back the memory of that day. She looked out of the window and reflected on the beauty of the afternoon. How empty she had been back then and without joy, like the house, she supposed.

Hannah closed her eyes, remembering the day as if looking back on a stranger.

She opened her eyes as a cool breeze entered the room, and a small child ran past and disappeared behind her

This time there was no emptiness, no ethereal figment but a golden-headed eight-year-old girl who slipped her hand easily into her own.

Smiling down at her daughter, they ran hand in hand from the room, down the steps, and into the sunshine.

The End

I started writing this story as part of a writing prompt on a writing course. We were given pictures of faces of people – cut out of magazines. Mine ended up being 'Geoffrey'!

Shades Of Grey

Geoffrey was a grey man of peculiar habits. He wore slip-on shoes and v necked sweaters in varying shades of casual beige.
By day he simpered behind a desk in an accountant's office. By night, he dreamed of lycra and the bronzed and toned bodies of fresh-faced young men with lips of crushed rose petals from which he longed to sip.

He lived alone with his mother in a two-up, two-down terrace. It was a nondescript street in an ordinary town, where the grime stained the cheeks of vacant-eyed children and layered the chiselled hollows of the old.

A collective, industrial tattoo.

Geoffrey's life was dull, a vast grim charcoal blanket edged with factory smog and dull steel. Emptiness and loneliness echoed and jarred like the desolate timbre of incidental music.

He was once mistaken for the ageing TV presenter Larry Spencer in an internet cafe. Someone had caused a scene, asking for an autograph. A skinny latte had been spilt, a computer ruined, and Geoffrey asked to leave. His five minutes of fame over before it had begun.

His mother was a large oily-skinned woman with an overbearing manner, and Geoffrey shrank from the mere sight. She bristled with sweat, brought on by the slightest exertion. The skin on her hands was dry and cracked, rubbed red and raw through years of working at the local launderette, a vile place smelling of cheap soap and gossip.

He loathed the way she ate her food sat opposite him, greasy-mouthed and salivating. A huge slobbering beast that could never be satiated, chomping through bones and gristle and vivid gelatinous mounds of fatty desserts.

Geoffrey hated his mother.

And now she had an idea. She had something in her head, something on her mind. And when his mother had an idea, it usually involved Geoffrey. It usually involved the idea of him getting married, for she never doubted the sexuality of her son and bullied him relentlessly on the subject.

His mother's idea was simple. She wanted to go on holiday for two weeks in June, and Geoffrey was to pay. She collected holiday brochures on her way back from the launderette, thick glossy tomes, oozing tanned skin and tropical skies, promising sun, sand, and sex. Geoffrey suggested Brighton. He had seen the advertisements for certain clubs in the magazines he kept locked in his bedside cabinet, away from his mother's prying eyes.

Mother had said Brighton was common, and anyway, she needed to go abroad for some sun.

Finally, she decided upon a cruise. She suggested the Caribbean and pursed her sticky lips when Geoffrey stated he could only stretch to twelve days in the Med. The quarrelsome mouth had flickered but remained silent, knowing when to keep her council. Besides, he might find a nice girl.

Geoffrey thought he would at least have some peace in the run-up to the holiday now that it was booked, but his mother had other ideas.

She was obsessed with their holiday wardrobe. She was a voracious shopper, and the holiday provided her with an additional excuse for squandering her minimum wage on the tatty and gaudy. She bought lurid plastic bangles, the colours bright and synthetic, cheap sandals that squashed her plump, bunioned feet.

She even bought a bathing suit, a remarkable feat of engineering in purple polyester that promised the illusion of a perfect figure. Geoffrey doubted that very much and tried not to look when his mother tried it on for him. As she paraded up and down the living room in the monstrosity, he felt sick. But the piece de résistance was saved for last. The brochure stated that there would be dinner with the Captain on the last night.

At least Geoffrey had shown interest in that! His mother bought a long evening dress in blue taffeta for the occasion, and he had to bite his lip. It was at least two sizes too small. How on earth was she to fit into it? His mother smiled, tapping a finger to her nose and giving Geoffrey a knowing smile. She had the very thing, *a wonder garment* made of thick Lycra and elastic that tucked and squeezed and lifted and separated.

This fantastic item of underclothing would solve all of her problems.

Now it was Geoffrey's turn. He didn't see anything wrong with his current wardrobe. His unhappy clothes suited his unhappy life. But his mother wouldn't let him be. He would embarrass her, having such a dowdy son. If he didn't go shopping, she would do it for him, and she did.

She bought cheap polyester Hawaiian shirts with pink palm trees and orange sunsets, green shorts and yellow T-shirts, and a pair of polka dot swimming trunks. Geoffrey said nothing, putting them into his case without trying them on, leaving ample room for his casual slacks and cardigans and the occasional cravat to add a little flair.

At last, the day arrived, after weeks of growing tension and more shopping. Handbags, magazines, sunglasses, sun cream, not forgetting the diarrhoea tablets. Just in case.

Geoffrey seemed to have a permanent headache.

But now they were here, on board the JOLLY VENTURE, a ship of vast proportions and overindulgence. A bit like his mother- thought Geoffrey. Their cabin was small yet comfortable. Twin beds. His mother had joked with the crew that Geoffrey was her toy boy.

Geoffrey managed a smile… only twelve days to endure. He groaned inwardly to himself. It might as well be a lifetime.

They unpacked quickly, his mother bemoaning the lack of a bath and the size of the bed. But she was enjoying herself already, fussing around the cabin, chastising Geoffrey for bringing his drab clothes.

The holiday progressed much the way Geoffrey expected. His mother spent hours in the sun, burning to a deep, unbecoming shade of lobster. She was usually asleep, sprawled out in her purple bather across a sun lounger, head lolled back, mouth open. Sometimes she looked as if she were dead. Geoffrey often looked for the rise and fall of her ample bosom to check she was still alive.

If only.

When not asleep, his mother was usually talking. Her broad northern accent was slightly clipped when in company, making her seem more common than usual. The conversation was typically about Geoffrey. Belittling and bullying, his mother talked about him, but never to him. He sat in silence, pretending to read. He was sure people thought him retarded, a single man living at home with his mother. He could see pity in their eyes and suspicion in others.

Geoffrey loathed his mother.

And then there was the food, in huge quantities; breakfast, lunch, afternoon tea, dinner, even snacks till the early hours.

His mother ate the lot.
Her greedy face chewed through egg and bacon, greasy fried bread, sausage, pies, curries, cream cakes, cheesecakes, ice creams, steaks, chips, and more chips. Her great cheeks filled, her lips constantly moist with the thought of her next meal. The oil and fat squeezed through her skin, mixing with the suntan lotion to give her a permanent unhealthy greasiness. The double chin quivered, her plump arms grew plumper, and her bathing costume strained and pulled at the seams -holding back the tide of blubber.

The days passed. Talking, eating, and drinking. Geoffrey grew more relaxed. He barely spoke but watched the fit, young Indian waiters stealthily behind his dark glasses.

The final night arrived, and the Captain's Party was soon upon them. Geoffrey's mother was beside herself at the thought of meeting the man himself and had somehow secured a seat at the Captain's table. Even Geoffrey was impressed. His mother laid out one of his Hawaiian shirts for the occasion, one of the more lurid, matched with purple jeans. He put them away, donning his usual beige and grey, though perhaps the red cravat tonight might add a little interest?

His mother was in the shower. He could hear the water gushing over her lumpy form. It was a wonder she could even fit inside the small enclosed space. He imagined the shower curtain sticking to her obesity, an image much more frightening than any Hitchcock film.

Emerging in a white towelling robe, her cheeks were red and flabby, hair thin and patchy. Glancing at his clothes, she opened her mouth to speak but turned away. She was not going to let Geoffrey spoil her evening.

His mother started disrobing, and Geoffrey immediately turned away. She had no idea of modesty.

"Oh Geoffrey, you're such a prude."

He winced as he thought of his mother naked, catching sight of her in the long wardrobe mirror.
What a view. Her legs, arms, and chest were crimson with the sun, burnt to a frazzle. Her middle was white, bleached against the red. What a look. She was disgusting. And now she was struggling into *the wonder garment*. Pulling and tugging and straining, she stuffed her rolls of fat into the tight lycra, her breathing shallow during the struggle. Several pounds heavier than when she arrived, she wrestled to fit into the elastic.

This was war, but Geoffrey bet on his mother and her grim determination.

Almost defeated, she lay on the bed, forcing her body inside. Mission completed, she wheezed herself slowly off the bed.

"Well, how do I look?" she questioned triumphantly.

Geoffrey turned around slowly. He had never seen anything so grotesque.

The undergarment had an interesting effect. It pushed and rolled her flab upwards, the spare being squeezed until everything was squashed together, giving the appearance of at least four breasts. At a loss for words, Geoffrey coughed and smiled.

His mother narrowed her eyes. "Don't spoil this for me, Geoffrey."

Slipping on the blue taffeta dress, it was tight against her bulging form. The neckline was low, emphasising the novelty of her strangely shaped bosom, but Geoffrey was past caring.

"Now, don't let me drink too much, Geoffrey, because I can't take this garment off easily- If you know what I mean. I don't want to get tiddly."

The time arrived, and they headed to the formal dining room to the Captain's table. Geoffrey lingered behind his mother, watching her hobble up the deck, staggering from side to side against the swell in her tight plastic sandals. Her feet were red and swollen, stretched against straps cutting red weals into her ankles where the cheap plastic met flesh.

The walk took less than five minutes, mostly by elevator, but Geoffrey's mother was already exhausted when she arrived at the foyer – just outside the main dining room. Her face was sweating, her makeup sliding away, mascara smudged, mouth drooping. But her eyes lit up as soon as she saw the Captain, dashing in his uniform.

She took a deep breath and walked over with an extended hand.

The Captain smiled his official smile, his eyes looking over the irregular chest with polite amusement. He shook her hand, now wet with perspiration, the chubby, ringed fingers squashed together in his firm grip as she simpered with delight. Geoffrey had never seen his mother simper, the large rough face trying its best to look coquettish, the hard eyes lowered in mock modesty.

She looked like a pig.

Geoffrey shook the hand of the Captain, firm and manly. Slightly blushing, he moved his mother quickly to find a seat.

The room was overcrowded and hot, full of bloated and burnt overdressed bodies. The pungent synthetic perfumes of the women blended into a potent, heady mix, causing his eyes to water.

The men coughed, and the ladies dabbed the powder from their perspiring pink faces. It would be 10 more minutes until they were seated in the dining room, and his mother pulled on his arm – eager for them to rest.

Geoffrey saw two empty seats in the far corner of the room and indicated his mother follow. She looked uncomfortable, swollen, her thick features contorting in the heat. Her breathing was heavy and laboured. She struggled to the seat, caught hold of the back of the chair for support, turned and twisted as if to sit, and then stopped.

She looked at Geoffrey, her eyes bulging.

"Sit down, Mother," Geoffrey held out his hand to assist.

His mother looked back at him with startled eyes, her mouth twisted in a grimace, her face turning purple. She opened her mouth to speak, but all she could manage was a choked gurgle.

"What on earth is the matter, Mother?" -Geoffrey stood up to help.

She was gasping for breath and trying to speak, her voice rasping, hardly audible.

"What was that, mother?"

The words, sporadic and unintelligible, bubbled from her mouth. Her hands tried to grasp at something, the stubby fingers reaching down the deformed neckline of the dress, trying to pull it away from her body.

Geoffrey looked at his mother. Her face pleaded back at him, mouth opening and closing yet silent for once save for the strangled gargling.

He looked at her hand groping around under the blue taffeta. She was trying to pull at something.

Then he realised. She was trying to pull at her underwear. The *wonder garment* must be too tight, and it was slowly squeezing the life out of her.

Geoffrey blinked; his mother seemed to be having some kind of fit.

The saliva was gathering in her mouth and bubbling, spilling out of the corners onto her ample chins.

He watched, amazed by the shades of purple her face was turning.

Geoffrey looked around. No one else seemed to have noticed.

Everyone was absorbed in their own conversations, wrapped in egos and champagne.

He looked back at his mother; she was turning a little blue around the mouth.

"Mother, are you alright?" Geoffrey tried to sound casual.

His mother looked back, her eyes large and rolling, popping from their sockets. She opened her mouth to speak, her tongue swollen and lolling, almost gagging her speech.

"PLEASE.....?"

They were her last words.

At least she had said please, the only time she had used that word in conversation with him.

With one last shake, her body slumped forward, lifeless across the table. The impact knocked one of the chairs sideways, but no one noticed the drama in the remote corner of the room. Perhaps he should fetch someone? He looked at his mother; it was too late for her now. Her eyes stared back at him, lifeless.

A dead, bloated fish.

He hoped the necessary formalities wouldn't take long. He had hoped to see that nice young man playing the piano on deck seven again.

The End

However unlikely the conclusion of this story sounds, it is indeed based on a true story- told to me by the person this happened to. The story and people are fictional - built around a real ending. They do say – you can't make it up!

Holiday Snaps

Angela and Ken were a smug couple. Friends or so-called friends nicknamed them Ken and Barbie, so perfect were their lives.

Ken ran his own business and made enough money for them to live a very comfortable lifestyle. He had worked himself up from used car salesman to being a dealer of luxury cars, the humble roots never referred to. He wore handmade suits and a wry smile, charm oozing from his permatan skin, topped up with the many holidays they took each year.

Angela worked in an office, in charge of several workers. Although the same age as the girls, Angela stood aloof from her team and treated her subordinates as an unruly mob to be kept under strict supervision. As a result, she was feared and disliked by those she managed. To those above, she proved sycophantic and gracious. She styled herself on Lady Di, her lifestyle icon, and had been inconsolable on her heroine's tragic death.

Angela dressed as a woman in her 50s rather than a woman in her 20s, wearing high-necked blouses with a large brooch at the throat, pearls, and tailored suits. Her hair was highlighted and cut short into a slight bouffant, held in precision by stiff hairspray.
Fully made up, even at weekends, Angela never had a hair out of place.

One could never imagine her reducing herself to the baser urges. Still, mindful of her matrimonial duties, she produced one son. He was a perfect golden-headed child called Harry, who would grow into a perfect young man, excelling in sports and academia and life itself.

So perfect were their lives that you would think them a rather dull subject to write about. Still, one incident told to me causes a smile every time I think about it, although it happened several decades ago. There is, after all, a universal justice!

The story takes place on one of their many holidays. The holidays were always luxurious; Hawaii, the Cayman Islands, St Kitts, Monaco, but this particular tale took place in America. The trip was a part holiday, part business. Ken was entertaining clients, and the first part of the trip took place in Los Angeles. It was summertime, and the heat was blistering. Wanting to keep up appearances, Angela had commissioned a five-piece suit in navy wool, trousers, skirt, dress, waistcoat, and jacket. During one event, she stood outside in the 40-degree heat wearing the whole combo.

In contrast, the rest of the ladies in the group wore strappy tops, shorts, and light dresses. Angela sneered at their informal dress; however, they formed a solid friendship and laughed behind her back, rejoicing at her obvious discomfort. Angela had not made any friends on the trip. Most of the women despised her airs and graces and only spoke to her when necessary.

The group flew to Hawaii the second week to spend a week's holiday. The resort was exclusive, and each couple was allocated a beachside residence with a sea view. Angela and Ken were the only couple to upgrade to their own private plunge pool and butler.

Even on holiday, Angela couldn't relax. She wouldn't lower herself to wear a common bikini but carefully chose designer slacks and a polo shirt. While Ken showed off his manly prowess, beating all the other men at water sports, she read a carefully selected novel. She had only read a few pages, it wasn't that interesting, but she had been told that this was THE author to follow. Knowing she had the cultural hand was enough, and she watched the other women strolling together, taking coffee and sunbathing without envy.

One day, taking pity on Angela, the other women asked if she would join them. They were going on a shopping expedition. For once, Angela agreed, accepting the invitation as graciously as a Queen accepts gifts from a commoner.

The girls set off using the shuttle bus from the hotel to take them into town. Angela was the last to get on the bus, choosing a seat by herself. The other girls chatted away excitedly at the prospect of spending their hard-earned money. Angela listened but kept quiet. Anne, a rather loud and brash girl, the exact opposite of Angela, both in looks and temperament, shouted across and asked what she would be buying. The girls were after cheap replicas of designer gear from the local shops. Angel smiled and cleared her throat. There were, she said, no genuine bargains, there was the cheap and the tatty, and then there was the expensive, designer, and well made. She would not be seen dead in anything fake but would head for the exclusive shopping area and check out the designer boutiques.

Anne rolled her eyes but, for once, kept quiet.

Arriving, the girls went one way to the cheap local shops, laughing and enjoying themselves, while Angela, erect in her dignity, set off for the designer quarter alone.

The girls were soon bitching about the high and mighty Angela. "She walks like she's got a poker shoved up her arse," Anne politely observed. "We need to wipe that smug smile off her face, and as for that husband of hers, he thinks he's God's gift, prancing about in his Speedo's, the budgie smuggler supremo!"

The opportunity to wipe the smugness from both Angela and Ken's faces arrived that very evening.

A group meal had been organised, but at the last minute, Ken and Angela decided to have a quiet, intimate dinner cooked by their own personal chef on a small uninhabited island not far from the resort.

As soon as the couple had set off in their private boat to their private dining experience, the girls started plotting, discussing what they might do. One mousey girl, who had been given a lecture on the art of makeup and making the most of herself by the perfect Angela, suggested breaking into their lodge and putting some of the giant local lizards into their beds. It was a popular suggestion!

Another, Rita, still smarting from an Angela put down, suggested that they break into their lodge to cut up her clothing. This proposal received a rousing cheer from the girls, but it was thought maybe a little extreme.

But it was the loud and raucous Anne who had the best idea.

When it was dark, the women strolled over to the lodge belonging to Ken and Angela. So exclusive was the resort that internal security was not thought necessary. The door was fastened with a simple catch, and the girls were soon inside to carry out their plan.

• • •

Early the following day, the group were having breakfast when Ken and Angela rushed over to join them – eager to speak. Someone had broken into their lodge the previous night, but nothing appeared to have been taken. However, the rooms, which were usually immaculate, were left a little untidy. Everyone looked up in surprised innocence, the girls glancing at each other. No one else had noticed anything; no one else had been burgled. Ken and Angela reported the incident to the hotel and were offered a complimentary champagne dinner at an exclusive restaurant for the inconvenience.

The matter was soon forgotten. Nothing had been stolen, and it looked like the golden couple had landed on their feet yet again.

The girls kept quiet. A collective secret kept them smiling throughout the rest of the holiday and immune to the haughty Angela.

• • •

A week later, they were back at home. Angela and Ken were glowing with health, their topped-up tans shown to advantage in clean, crisp white shirts and blouses.

On the first Wednesday back, after a rather splendid dinner and a fine bottle of wine, the couple settled back to look through the holiday photographs. Ken had picked them up earlier from the prompt service at the local chemist.

Ah, for those halcyon pre-digital days.

Smiling the whitest of expensive smiles, they flicked through the snaps. There they were - raising champagne glasses with a sunset backdrop, Ken in trunks looking handsome and tanned, Angela reposing in perfect recline on a sun lounger.

The following few photos were blurry, poorly shot, dark, and out of focus. They both peered, thinking they had received someone else's poor efforts by mistake, when Ken noticed one of the inside of their lodge. Yes, it was definitely their holiday lodge.

What followed caused those perfect smiles to quiver. The next picture was clearly in focus.

In the centre of the photograph were two large bare bottoms bent over, quite in focus, and clearly inserted into each of the offending orifices were two designer toothbrushes, his and hers, bristles first.

I heard Angela fainted!

The End

Another story that started from a writing prompt. Probably inspired by reading too many of Roald Dahl's short stories!

Ethel Nobody Has Her Day

Ethel Nobody wanted something exciting to happen. She prayed for some event in her life, anything.

Every morning and every evening, she knelt and asked God for one significant moment in her life, to be somebody.

She put her trust in God and knew that her prayers would be answered one day. Of course, 'Ethel Nobody' wasn't her real name, but it may as well have been. She had no friends, no relations. She was a nobody.

Her life had been very dull and drab, a nobody's kind of life. Her early childhood had been lonely and loveless. Her parents had died when she was five, and she was left in the care of her Mother's sister, her Aunt Mabel, and her husband, Fred. They had no children of their own and resented the intrusion of having their niece thrust upon them in such macabre and disagreeable fashion.

As soon as possible, Mabel and Fred sent Ethel to boarding school, a very austere and dreary place but quite economical on the pocket.

Ethel was a mousy, quiet, unattractive girl. The unfortunate type picked on by other girls and never the teacher's pet. Her limp hair would never hold a curl, and she was tall for her age and quite clumsy.

At first, she had been a novelty, a freak, someone to be bullied and teased in the playground, but Ethel never retaliated. She never spoke harshly back to the other girls, and their games soon grew dull, and Ethel was left alone in her own world.

She knew that one day something would happen. Her mother had told her, so it must be true.

If she was a good girl and said her prayers, Jesus would answer them.

Her prayers were concerned with one topic that she, Ethel Nobody, a tall, gangly, mousy girl, would have her day. Like the heroines in the picture books, the princess awaiting her prince, the orphan adopted by a wealthy old gentleman, the ugly duckling that grew into a beautiful swan.

Yes, one day, Ethel's prayers would be answered. Her mother had promised.

And so Ethel travelled through life in a dull grey way, keeping hope, like Pandora, contained in a box hidden deep inside her and far away from the hurt and pain of the world.

Having left school at 15, she went straight into employment, working as both housekeeper and part-time governess to a rather large and balding mill owner and his spoilt daughter.

Rather than turning into a Charlotte Bronte heroin, Ethel became a skivvy of the lowest order, scrubbing and cleaning, making and serving meals from dawn until dusk, pausing only to try and educate young Beatrice in the rudiments of the three Rs. Her reward was a meagre wage and harsh words.

Beatrice had been a petulant child, hissing and spitting when she didn't get her own way. Ethel endured all through patient and gentle eyes, for she was sure in the hope that one-day salvation would be hers and that her life would change.

One day!

There had been several jobs after the mill owner. She had tried her hand at being a governess again, but children did not seem to warm to her. It was during this period, on her afternoon off, when, reading a newly purchased copy of The Lady magazine Ethel came across the following advert:

"Wanted: Female wanted for exciting opportunity - no qualifications required: Live in - permanent position: Solid, mature plain woman preferred with no family obligations. Some travel involved. Please enclose a small photograph with details of height, weight, and age. Photograph– non-returnable"

Ethel was drawn to the advert. At 55, she was definitely mature and most definitely plain. The only daunting thing about the advert was the photograph.

Ethel had a few pictures of herself as a child, creased and sepia-toned in the back of a drawer somewhere.

She just hadn't needed a photograph of herself.

Why would she? If she'd been a great beauty, even mildly attractive, it might have been pleasant having a small photograph, a keepsake for the next generation, but that wasn't the case.

Anyway, there wouldn't be a 'next-generation.' When Ethel died, there would be no one to carry on the bloodline.

But not to be deterred, Ethel woke early the following day, washed her thinning hair, and dusted powder on her face. She looked at herself in the mirror. She had pulled her hair back into a bun, making her face seem severe. The powder clumped in the lines around her eyes, making her look old and ghoulish. Still, it was an improvement, she thought and set off on the brisk three-mile walk into town to Mr Ambrose's Photographic Studio. The process didn't take long, and soon she owned a small head and shoulder image that had cost 1 shilling. Mr Ambrose had been worried that Ethel wouldn't be pleased with the finished result as he had handed over the unflattering portrait, but Ethel had come to terms with her face and was quite happy that the picture didn't show all her wrinkles.

On returning home, she quickly wrote back to the post box number quoted in the advertisement, slipping the photograph between the folded reply.

This might be it, she thought excitedly. *This could be my time!*

Ethel prayed hard that night. Although she still had hope, the years of hardship had made it difficult to keep believing something exciting would happen, something that would make people sit up and notice.

Ethel could not have expected such a timely response even with her hope and prayers. She received a letter asking for an interview by the next day's post and was to call the following day at the address mentioned at 2 pm sharp.

Ethel was all of a dither. The hope within her now flickered into a glowing certainty.

This was it.

She could hardly sleep that night and lay beneath the thin blankets, her heart beating with childish excitement. The words of the advertisement whirling around and around.

Exciting opportunity; some travel.

Travel!

Ethel had never travelled more than 10 miles from her place of birth, not counting the 25 miles she had travelled to school. She might even see the sea or travel abroad. Ethel could hardly think of the possibilities opening up before her and uttered a special heartfelt prayer not to be disappointed.

The following day she rose early, even though the appointment was not until the afternoon. She dressed in her best skirt and blouse and put on her coat. She was rather ashamed of her coat, two of the buttons didn't match, and it was rather threadbare on one sleeve. Still, it was all she had, and the advert had stated a 'plain' woman was required. She looked at herself in the small crazed mirror she kept on a set of drawers and sighed.

Yes, she was undoubtedly plain.

But she was about to become a 'somebody' of that she was certain.

The clock struck a quarter to one. Ethel had been ready and sat in her coat and hat for an hour. It would take her an hour to walk to the address. It was a fine day, and after the expense of the photograph, Ethel didn't want the added cost of a tram ticket.

Besides, she was so excited that she didn't want to wait for a second longer. The walk would calm her nerves. Grabbing her gloves and bag, she almost danced out of the doorway into the street beyond with a new lightness. Her feet didn't seem to touch the pavement; it was as if she was walking on air. Even the neighbours gave Ethel a second glance as she skipped down the drab grey street.

The sun shone weakly through the November skies, the day was bitterly cold, but Ethel hardly noticed. The thought of a new life was keeping her warm. Part of the journey took her through the great park, a magnificent legacy of a past king once preserved for Royal shoots, but now the majestic oaks and limes swayed over the rich and common alike.

Ethel kicked her way amongst the fallen leaves, delighting as a child as they crunched underfoot.

 Her heart thudded. A trapped bird, at last, about to escape the confining hand of her dreary life.

This was it, this was it.

She arrived in the street shown on the address. A quiet, neat place just off the main road, consisting of several modest two-storey terraced houses with steps leading up to the front door. She counted down the row: 2, 4, 6, 8, 10. Number 10 was the place. A neat-looking house, well cared for, she thought, a black door with a brass knocker and nets at the window.

Ethel looked at her watch, five minutes to two. She took a deep breath and began to climb the steps of number 10. Pausing for a moment, on the threshold of her new life, a wave of mixed emotions flooded her mind, excitement, and apprehension for what lay beyond.

She carefully lifted her hand to raise the knocker.

Inside number 10, Mr Taylor was in an upstairs room. He looked at himself in the mirror and adjusted his tie. Five to 2, nearly time for his appointment. He examined his face peering closely at the mirror through tiny round spectacles. His balding head reflected the light from the window, his brow beaded slightly with sweat. He was very excited about his latest venture. His hands twitched with excitement, and his stubby fingers drummed the long table in front of him.

Everything was in place. Edward liked to keep a tight ship, everything neat and tidy.

He looked through the net curtain briefly and saw a woman across the way. Surely that must be her, Ethel. He hoped so.

A fine specimen, so tall; the skeleton would be tremendous, just what Dr Tremaine was looking for on his latest European tour. He stopped to adjust a row of surgical knives, lining them up neatly, all newly sharpened and gleaming.

Now, to put the kettle on. A nice cup of tea was required before settling down to business.

The End

It's funny where you get inspiration from. A short tale based on memories of a 1970's carpet.

Ayin Harsha (Evil Eye)

The funeral had already taken place. A quiet formality that had been a fair reflection of a life lived and now no more.

Some lives can be full and extraordinary, and yet short. Mum had lived a long uneventful life. As long as I had been aware, she had been housebound. Nothing physical, but a crippling mental shadow that had closed the doors on her life- literally. For as long as I could remember, Mum had been agoraphobic.

The word agoraphobia is derived from Greek words, meaning 'fear of the marketplace'. The term describes an irrational and often disabling fear of being out in public.

For the last 40 years, she had never left the house. As a child, I had accepted this without question, dad or friends meeting me from school. Yet, as I grew, I noticed how different my life was. No day trips with mum and dad, no mum and daughter shopping. Teenage angst made me feel angry toward her, but as I grew older, I became more sympathetic.

As far as I could tell, Mum had been a normal child. I'd seen the faded and creased black and white photographs from the mid-20s and early 30s. She'd transformed from a shy smiling toddler to a carefree pre-war teenager to a beautiful woman. Yes, Mum had definitely been a beauty. Her heart-shaped face, dark hair, and brown eyes would have made her a classic beauty in any era, like her mother before her, another great beauty of her time.

Pity I took after my father!

Mum had been courted and married by my father at the age of 19, coinciding with the close of the Second World War.
He was a handsome and charming young man who had served in the army and seen the last few years of the war unscathed, returning quite quickly to civilian life.

They'd met at a dance while he was home on leave, and within 18 months, they were married. They had managed to buy a small house on my father's accountant's wage and lived happily in post-war suburbia. The only blot on their seemingly peaceful world was the lack of a child.

It would be 17 years later when they had almost given up hope that I was born.

Those early years in the 1960s with a baby seem tranquil, reflected in the camera's gaze. Dad had been successful in his career, and the small house had now become a large detached rambling pile in the country. There are images of picnics on the lawn, birthday parties and Christmas, and most of all, happiness.

All of this seemed to change when my Mothers mum, my grandma, died.

There had been nothing to suggest any mental health issues with my mother until this point. Of course, there had been family history.

My Grandmother started with mental health problems following her early marriage in 1903 at the age of 18 to my grandfather, 20 years her senior. Grandpa had served in India in the 46th Punjabis until an illness had forced him back to England. He had been friends with my Great Grandfather and met my Grandmother on a visit to the house.

He was immediately smitten by this beautiful young creature. Flattered by the attentions of an older man, along with encouragement from her father, she was married within 6 months of their meeting.

The wedding, by all accounts, was a lavish Edwardian affair, my great grandfather being a respected doctor. Having never really known my Grandmother, I often scoured her wedding photos, looking for a clue.

The beautiful heart-shaped face framed by lace looking eagerly and expectantly into the future.

My grandfather older, with some of the Victorian stiffness and sternness etched on his face.

I never knew him. He died 7 years before I was born. I often wondered what he had been like. Had he driven my Grandmother to some kind of breakdown? My mother spoke of him as a kind and generous man, proud and possessive of his beautiful young bride.

He'd been a good father, bringing her up and acting as both parents. Grandmother had been around but mainly confined to her bedroom.

Within a few months of their marriage, Grandmother suffered paranoia and delusions. My mother said she thought she was being watched, and a slow reluctance to socialise and undertake everyday tasks led to hysteria and an aversion to stepping into the outside world, even outside of her own bedroom.

 The birth of her daughter served only to pull her more deeply into her confinement.

That's how I remember my Grandmother, a prisoner in her own bedroom. She was usually lying on her bed with the curtains closed, too tired for life, too afraid. I was brought in as a child sporadically when she was feeling 'better' to lighten the mood. I can clearly remember being set down on the floor to play while my mother spoke in soothing tones.

I barely remember anything of those times. The only lasting memory is of the beautiful Persian carpet set at the foot of the bed. As a young child, I had been fascinated by the exquisite colours, lost in the jewelled spectacle and softness of the wool.

My grandfather had brought the carpet from Arabia as a gift to his bride as a wedding present. He'd been keenly interested in Eastern folklore during his army days, and it was said that the design on the carpet represented fidelity in marriage and showed his love and commitment to his new wife.

Grandfather didn't have to worry about the faithfulness of his young and beautiful bride.

Her mental deterioration would keep her indoors and away from admiring glances for the rest of her life.

The cause of my Grandmother's illness was never explained or fully explored. Doctors wanted to commit her to an asylum, but my grandfather could not think of his precious package subjected to the known horrors of the Edwardian Asylum, so he cared for her at home.

He looked after her until his death. My mother continued as chief carer until grandma died, aged 85, in 1970.

By the time of my Grandmother's death, my mother was 45 years old. Up to that point, she had shown no signs of mental imbalance.

Yet within 12 months of her mother dying, she too was confined to her room, hardly daring to venture downstairs and never leaving the house.

And now she was dead too.

My dad was now in his late 80s, and although in good shape, my mother's death hit him hard. We decided that it would be better if he was looked after in a nursing home with 24-hour care. With Mum only dead a month and Dad looking frail and lost, I found it hard to keep strong and positive for him.

I took on the responsibility of sorting out the house for Dad and getting it ready to sell. It took a couple of weeks to go through all the cupboards and shelves, boxing up books and knick-knacks. A lifetime of objects, papers, and photographs rifled through in haste.

The fate of once-cherished items decided in seconds; some to be swept away to the charity shops or, worse still, taken to the council tip.

After a particularly long afternoon sorting through boxes, I went upstairs and sat on my mother's bed.

The room had been her world for nearly 40 years. I glanced through the window onto the long lawn and rosebushes that must have brought joy during her confined years. My eyes drifted along the walls, past photographs, and pictures. The dressing table, her brush, comb, mirror, and jewellery box all gathering dust in the afternoon light.

The dressing table mirror caught my reflection. At 47 years of age, I was greying at the temples and looking tired. I was already middle-aged and frumpy without my mother's or grandmother's looks.

Something bright caught my attention in the corner of the room. It was the old Persian Carpet. Unlike me, the carpet looked as bright and fresh as the day it was bought. I turned and brushed my hand over the soft pile bringing back memories of long-forgotten afternoons in my Grandmother's bedroom.

After she died, my mother brought the carpet back as an heirloom. And now Mum was gone, the carpet would be mine. I gazed at the colours and the patterns weaving and winding in and out. I traced the patterns with my fingers round and round, others like exotic flowers bursting in the Arabian heat. There was some uniformity, some subtle plan to this design. All the swirls and curls swept to the centre of the carpet. The detail formed part of a larger, much more complex shape.

I stood, stepping back to view the design from a distance. It seemed...yes, I was sure...most definitely; the exotic pattern formed the shape of an elaborate eye.

As I looked deeper and deeper into the pattern, the shapes and colours swam before me, sweeping me deeper and deeper into the hypnotic gaze.

And briefly, for a moment, a sudden fear swept over me, chilling me to the core… as if I could never walk away...

The End

Printed in Great Britain
by Amazon

79112921R00088